BE

Christine couldn't understand why such a man as Richard Kingsley should want to bury himself in an isolated house in Scotland. And when she did find out why, she also discovered that she couldn't leave him there on his own, even if his fiancée could . . .

Books you will enjoy
by MARGARET PARGETER

IMPASSE

Five years after they had parted, Lee Moreau and Slade Western had met again—and Lee soon realised that all her old love for Slade had come back, too. But now she was engaged to nice, kind Matt Leland. How could she hurt him by leaving him for a man who wasn't even offering her marriage?

LOST ENCHANTMENT

Eden resolved that Dane, her estranged husband, should know all about their six-year-old son, Jonathan—the son he had never even seen. But how would that affect her and Dane?

THE OTHER SIDE OF PARADISE

Vicky couldn't share in Nick Rawdon's deception, nor bear the pain of his constant rejection. Their passion was heaven, but his paradise had a serpent, unseen but with a venom too deadly for love to survive . . .

BEYOND REACH

BY

MARGARET PARGETER

MILLS & BOON LIMITED
15–16 BROOK'S MEWS
LONDON W1A 1DR

First published in Great Britain 1986
by Mills & Boon Limited

This edition 1986

ISBN 0 263 75338 7

Set in Monophoto Times 10 on 10 pt.
01–0486 – 58063

Made and printed in Great Britain by
Richard Clay (The Chaucer Press) Ltd,
Bungay, Suffolk

CHAPTER ONE

CHRISTINE heard the knocking on the door as she woke up. It must have awakened her.

'Who on earth?' she mumbled aloud, becoming aware of several things at once as she opened her eyes, and liking none of them. She saw, by the way the sun was high in the sky, that she should have been up hours ago, and felt how stiff her face was from the amount of make-up she had plastered on the night before and had forgotten to wash off before retiring. Her mouth felt terrible, too, because of the quantity of wine she had drunk at the party. It must have been the wine, though she'd had only two glasses but she wasn't used to it. Or maybe it was all the rich food she had eaten? She hadn't been accustomed to too much of that lately, either.

Rolling out of bed naked, she reached for her dressing-gown and shivered as the thin material provided little protection against the chill of the early morning. As soon as summer was gone and the first winds of autumn blew down the glen and over the loch, the weather quickly became colder.

With another groan of protest against the increasingly thunderous knocking, she sped downstairs, fearing whoever was outside was in danger of breaking the door down. Could it be Ken, come back to help clear up the mess left by the party? He had offered to but she had refused and it was unlike him to remember anything as mundane as unwashed dishes.

'All right, I'm coming!' she called, struggling with the rusty key in the heavy lock. Immediately she managed to turn it, the door flew open, which made her realise that the person knocking had also been turning the knob. The man who stood there, though, wasn't Ken or anyone remotely like him. He was a stranger.

He was tall with startling green eyes and jet black hair and the dark overcoat he wore emphasised the powerful width of his shoulders. In the seconds that passed as she stared at him speechlessly, she noticed that he looked pale and slightly haggard and also very angry. As their eyes met she fancied he would have enjoyed knocking her out of his way, as he might have done a fly.

But it was something else about the man that made her feel unaccountably nervous. Suddenly she realised it was the manner in which he appeared to dominate everything, even the rugged scenery behind him, without saying a word.

'Who—are you?' she whispered, drawing the shabby folds of her robe closer about her, as if seeking its protection.

Their eyes locked and Christine could feel something peculiar passing between them, but if the man felt anything he ignored it. He also ignored her uncertain query as he pushed past her over the threshold, as if he owned the place.

Perhaps he did? Christine turned and began shaking in horror as it swiftly dawned on her that he could be the man whom she had been informed, two weeks ago, might be coming from the firm who had bought Cragend. She hadn't heard from them since the sale had been completed until then, and when the days had passed without anyone turning up, she had presumed that whoever had been coming had changed their mind.

'Are you from the people who took over Cragend?' she asked apprehensively as he glanced sharply around.

'I am,' he confirmed curtly. 'And I didn't expect to be welcomed like this.' Again he surveyed the untidiness of the hall, the discarded plates, scattered cups and left-over food. He looked far from impressed.

'I—I had a few friends in last night,' Christine stammered. She didn't know how to explain, or if she could without making matters worse, and she wished again that she had cleared everything up before going to bed.

'It wouldn't take a lot of intelligence to guess that you hadn't been celebrating alone,' the man said sarcastically. 'However,' he shrugged, 'I'd be obliged if, before you start clearing up, you would call the housekeeper.'

'I—I am the housekeeper. Christine Colwell.'

The hard face in front of her went even grimmer. 'Little girl,' he drawled, 'I've been travelling half the night, I'm in no mood for playing games. Just call the lady I asked for, will you? Unless,' his eyes returned with contempt to the chaos about them, 'like you, she enjoyed the party too well and is still in a drunken stupor.'

Christine's small, slender body went rigid with a fury she couldn't contain. 'How dare you come here and speak to me like this?' she gasped.

'The housekeeper!'

So, he meant to ignore her anger! Christine tensed but, remembering her position, managed to control herself. 'I tell you, I am the housekeeper,' she persisted. 'If you don't believe me, all you have to do is ring your firm. They bought the house from my stepmother as a sort of holiday home for their staff, and they said I could stay on to look after it and the staff when they arrived.'

'Good God!' Green eyes darkened with a temper as quick as her own. 'Did no one check?'

'Check?'

'On your suitability!' he snapped, as if it was another black mark against her that she should have to ask. 'You're far too young and irresponsible; too just about everything on the minus side, I should imagine.'

'Looks can be deceiving,' Christine said, as evenly as she could.

'Young woman,' the severity of the man's tone matched his eyes, 'I've had too many people through my hands to be deceived by anyone.'

Christine hesitated on a sharply drawn breath. She needed a roof over her head and the one above her seemed in danger of disappearing. Instead of losing her temper it might pay her to try and reason with him. Painfully she bit on the tongue that was inclined to be too hasty.

'What you are seeing,' she said earnestly, 'isn't a true reflection of either the house or me.'

'Really?' he said disparagingly.

Christine watched him warily. Contrary to her overall impression of him, he looked like a man under considerable strain. Something was bothering him and while she was suddenly sure it wasn't her, she was reluctant to be used as a scapegoat.

'Would you mind waiting in the lounge until I get dressed?' she asked. 'Then we can talk.' Without waiting for his reaction to that, she sped hastily to the lounge and opened the door. 'This way,' she said politely.

The bleak eyes didn't soften, especially when the lounge unfortunately proved to be no tidier than the hall, but if she had been surprised at her own audacity, she was even more surprised when, without protesting, he merely walked past her and sank into the nearest chair. Leaning back, he closed his eyes and rubbed a weary hand over his head.

'You'll have a fire and breakfast immediately,' she promised rashly, keeping her fingers crossed that there would be enough dry logs and sufficient food.

Thankful that he seemed in a more amenable mood, she cast one more glance at the silent figure in the chair and raced upstairs. In her room, she washed and dressed faster than she could ever recall doing in her life and was down again within a few minutes. Her dark hair curled naturally and only required a few quick flicks with a brush, while her pink-and-white complexion was so clear and healthy it didn't need any make-up to replace that which she had washed off. Wearing a skirt and T-shirt under a primly buttoned overall, she hoped she looked more responsible. She forgot about her bare feet, thrust carelessly into a pair of old sandals.

The man was still in the lounge but no longer sitting down. As if regretting a momentary weakness, he was prowling around looking more ferocious than ever. Wishing she could make herself invisible, Christine knelt furtively by the fireplace with an armful of dry logs.

'Would you mind explaining what you are doing?' he asked icily.

'Lighting a fire.'

'Were you really serious when you said you were the housekeeper?' he snapped.

'Yes.'

In a flash she was hauled to her feet, within inches of a pair of glittering eyes. Both the swiftness of his actions and the way his eyes rayed into her did something disturbing to her breathing.

'If you think I'm willing to accept you as anything, then you are greatly mistaken,' he ground out. 'You can go and pack and leave this house immediately.'

If Christine had been trembling before, she was visibly shaking now. 'I can't do that!' she croaked, as he almost flung her from him. 'Where would I go?'

'Relatives,' he clipped. 'You must have some.'

She shook her head speechlessly.

'What about the stepmother you mentioned?'

Christine gulped. 'I haven't heard from her since my father died and she sold the house. I believe she's with her new husband in America.'

'Join them,' he advised indifferently. 'Best place for you. I don't care where you go, as long as it's out of my sight. You're not my responsibility anyway.'

'Oh, please!' She raised pleading blue eyes to his cold ones.

'Not another word!' Catching hold of her thin shoulders again, he turned her ruthlessly in the direction of the stairs. 'You can leave as quickly as you like. I'm too hardened a character to be taken in by any sob-story. I don't employ people who are so obviously inefficient but if you can prove that you were hired by us, I'll pay you a month's wages in lieu of notice.'

How long would that take? With an indignant gasp, Christine wrenched free of him and fled. Upstairs, she rushed into her room and collapsed on the bed. Her hands curled into fists as she thought of the man she had just left. Just who did he think he was? And, come to think of it, who exactly was he? He hadn't introduced himself, so how could she be sure he had any authority to throw her out? Wouldn't it be wiser, before she went, to ring the firm who had bought the house and see if he really was able to dismiss her?

Her courage returning, she was about to go and do that when she suddenly realised she had no number to ring. The only confirmation of her employment had been the one small cheque she had received before they had apparently forgotten about her. She had heard nothing more until they had rung to say someone was coming. Anyway, she conceded, her newly found courage fading, the man downstairs looked as if he might have a lot more say in the matter than anyone she might try to get in touch with.

Threading agitated fingers through her mop of unruly curls, she tried desperately to reassess her position. The small amount of money she'd saved when her father died had almost gone; she might not have enough in her purse to get her as far as even Inverness. Still—she got to her feet with a helplessly resigned shrug—nothing would be achieved by sitting here feeling sorry for herself.

Not being sure that there was such a thing as a suitcase left in the house, she found two carrier bags and began stuffing her clothes into them. Maybe Jamie Angus at the other end of the loch would be willing to put her up for a few nights, until she decided what to do.

Never having expected to leave Cragend quite like

this, she was so busy trying to control the tears which sprang to her eyes that she didn't hear the man come into the room. She had no idea of his presence until he touched her.

'Oh!' She almost jumped out of her skin as she swung around. 'I'm being as quick as I can . . .

'You can stop what you are doing for the moment,' he cut in curtly.

'You told me to get out.'

'My memory isn't that short,' he retorted. 'You will be leaving, but not before you've cleared up the mess you've made and cooked me some breakfast. I don't see why anyone but you should have to do it.'

'I was going to put everything straight as soon as I got up, Mr . . .'

'Kingsley.'

'Mr Kingsley.' Slowly she repeated his name, then to her dismay she found herself gabbling. 'A friend arrived last night, with some friends. It was his birthday . . .'

Her words might have fallen on deaf ears. 'I don't need an explanation, Miss Colwell. I can guess for myself what has been going on while there's been no one here to keep an eye on you.'

'I'll begin clearing up right away.'

'No.' His mouth thinned at her mutinous expression. 'I'll have some breakfast first, if you don't mind. You can see to the other while I'm eating.'

Christine tried to hide her anger and look meek as she swept past him and ran down to the kitchen. Unfortunately she tripped on the ragged carpet in the hall and landed flat on her face before she reached it. Damn the man, she thought, as rough hands dragged her to her feet again.

'Try walking, you might get there faster.' Looking into her furious eyes, his own narrowed mockingly. 'No use getting in a temper with me, my girl. If you aren't satisfied with the way things have turned out, you have only yourself to blame.'

Christine could no longer contain herself. 'Wouldn't

you be upset,' she exploded, 'if you thought you were working for a firm and then suddenly found yourself thrown out without notice? Come to think of it,' she challenged bravely, 'what right have you to come here and dictate to me? What authority do you have to terminate my employment?'

The green eyes continued mocking. 'All the authority in the world, Miss Colwell. You see, I happen to own the firm which mistakenly employed you. In other words, I'm the boss.'

'Y-you are?'

He nodded.

Looking at him, she suddenly didn't doubt it, yet something perverse made her persist. 'You can prove it?'

'Ring my office, or better still, here's my passport.' His hand delved in a pocket. 'I've just returned from Brazil.'

She only glanced at his passport long enough to note that his first name was Richard and shook her head when he began quoting a London number. 'What I can't understand is what are you doing at Cragend? I was under the impression that it had been purchased as a sort of holiday home for your employees.'

'That may be so, Miss Colwell,' he agreed with a suddenly shuttered expression. 'But exactly why it was purchased need no longer concern you. I'd appreciate it more if you would just get on with my breakfast.'

The kitchen was large and cosy and fairly well equipped but Richard Kingsley didn't spare it any compliments. He would be too busy looking for something to criticise, she thought morosely, filling up the kettle and plugging it in.

'I prefer coffee,' he said, sitting down at the table and watching her so closely that she wondered if he thought she was about to make off with something.

For the first time, she noticed that he had discarded his overcoat and that he was wearing a soft cashmere pullover underneath. The fine black wool, pushed into a pair of casual black trousers and secured to his lean waist by a black leather belt, made him suddenly look diabolically attractive. Christine gulped, without knowing why, as a peculiar feeling shot through her again.

'I'm sorry, there isn't any coffee,' she said quickly. 'Just tea.'

'Which more than illustrates your capabilities as a housekeeper,' he murmured sarcastically. 'What else have you forgotten to order?'

'It's not a case of forgetting to order, Mr Kingsley,' she retorted sharply. 'I was only told that someone might be coming and given no authority to order anything. Your firm should have thought of that.'

'It's not an oversight that can't be rectified,' he said smoothly, infuriating Christine afresh that he was willing to overlook the mistakes of his staff but not hers. 'I'll have fresh supplies delivered immediately, but surely you keep something in the house?'

'I manage on very little,' she replied stiffly, wondering what he would say if he knew just how little she had managed on during the past weeks.

'Have you been paid at all for your services?' he asked suddenly.

'For a month, at the beginning,' she revealed reluctantly, incensed by his sarcasm.

Folding his arms across the breadth of his chest, he stared at her disapprovingly. 'So instead of doing something about it, as any logical person would have, you sat here and sulked.'

'No, that's not true!' Indignantly she banged a cup and saucer down before him. 'I needed this job, Mr Kingsley, and I wanted to keep it, but I had no idea who to get in touch with.'

'No address?'

'Just your firm's name which was included with the cheque.'

'That would have found me.'

'How was I to know?'

He sighed, as if she was an unknown quantity he

hadn't come across before. 'Never mind,' he said impatiently. 'It's not worth arguing about. As for food, I feel so hungry, I'd be grateful for even a slice of toast.'

Opening the larder door, Christine looked around anxiously. Apart from a piece of home-cured bacon, which wasn't to everyone's taste, and a few eggs, there was nothing. With a wry grimace, she removed the bacon from its hook and began cutting it into thick slices. When it was nearly cooked she broke three eggs into the pan beside it, thinking resignedly that as she could hardly take them with her, he may as well have them.

All the time she was busy, she was aware of the unfriendly green eyes studying her. She guessed that his thoughts would be far from flattering, but then she wouldn't be the kind of girl a man like him would normally even notice. She was only five-foot-four and too thin, with nondescript features; unless, as her stepmother had been fond of taunting, you liked Irish blue eyes, a tilted nose and a mouth that was too wide for a small face.

'What's this?' Mr Kingsley's deep voice broke through her thoughts as she set the bacon and eggs in front of him.

'Your breakfast, of course.' She glanced at him in bewilderment.

'I can see what it is, but what is it?'

'Bacon.' She frowned, thinking enviously of the feast he was about to have, comparing it with the meagre allowance she allowed herself each morning.

'Looks extremely fat to me.'

'It tastes wonderful though,' she said stoutly, as he peered at it suspiciously before picking up his cutlery.

After pouring his tea and making toast, she excused herself to get on with the tidying up. She didn't bother with a cup of tea for herself, being only too glad to get away from those glinting eyes, narrowed in disapproving contemplation.

In the hall she paused and looked around with a sigh.

She had to admit that Richard Kingsley had some room for complaint. Ken had certainly left a mess behind him. If she had known he was coming she would have stopped him but she had found it impossible to turn away one of the few friends she had when he had arrived on the doorstep with a car-load of friends and refreshments. They had even brought gaily coloured decorations—wryly she began gathering them up. The various selections of delicatessen food, along with pies and pizzas which just needed warming up had proved irresistible to a girl who usually survived on next to nothing.

After burning the paper in the huge fireplace in the lounge, she stacked the dirty plates and glasses on a trolley, working diligently until everything was restored to order. Cragend was only a moderately sized house but it rambled. There were five bedrooms upstairs, and downstairs, apart from the dining-room, kitchen and lounge there was only a small study and one or two other rooms which were never used. She glanced sadly towards the study, where her father had done his writing, which she had typed for him.

Cragend was solidly comfortable but that was about all that could be said for it, and, no matter how hard she tried, she couldn't think of anything about it that might provide her with a clue as to why Richard Kingsley had come here. When Leila, her stepmother, had written to say she had sold Cragend to a firm as a holiday home, she had decided they must have bought it as a kind of experiment. She had read about big organisations sending their executive staff on outdoor courses as a therapeutic answer to stress, but the one man who had arrived didn't somehow seem to support such a theory. Yet why would anyone wish to come here otherwise? The house was set in about a hundred acres along the side of a loch, but most of the ground was sheer crag and forest, some of which was too rough even to walk on. The view across the loch was spectacular on a clear day but no one could deny that it was lonely. Some might not consider ten miles from the nearest village and sixty from Inverness, too isolated; but to Christine—though she loved it—Cragend might have been on another planet, so remote did it sometimes seem from the rest of the world. She found it difficult to understand what a man like Richard Kingsley was doing here.

She waited until he emerged from the kitchen before she went in with the dirty dishes. He didn't speak as she passed him but went straight into the lounge.

He may have eyed the food she had provided with little enthusiasm but he had eaten everything apart from a few scraps. These she scraped carefully into a bowl which she carried to the back door. She had forgotten about Wolf, the old mongrel dog who occasionally called for a meal when he couldn't find anything else. He was well known in the glen and nobody minded him but on very cold nights he seemed to favour Cragend, perhaps because Christine let him sleep in the big warm kitchen.

He would find no favour with Mr Kingsley, she sighed, hiding the bowl where she hoped he wouldn't see it. Anything as ill-bred as Wolf would be beneath his notice. She would have to remember to tell Jamie to give him a little extra after she was gone.

The dishes washed and put away neatly, she returned to her room to continue her packing. Now that she had finished being angry with Richard Kingsley and wondering about him, the precariousness of her own position returned to haunt her. Even if Jamie could put her up for a few days, that was really no answer. Where could she go from there? What would she do? If it had been summer, she might have found employment in an hotel, but at this time of the year there was little likelihood of that.

She was taking a last look around to make sure she hadn't left anything and was about to pick up her carrier bags, when Richard Kingsley pushed his head around her door again.

'I'd like to talk to you. Would you mind coming downstairs?'

What more could he have to say to her? Following him reluctantly, she wondered why his former brusqueness had been replaced by something surprisingly resembling politeness.

He turned to face her in the hall and suddenly she knew how his staff must feel when he confronted them at a board meeting. He was one of the kind her father used to tell her about. Steely eyes that never missed a thing and a tongue which boded ill for anyone discovered guilty of anything which displeased him. Well, in another few minutes she would be gone, so whatever he disliked about her, which seemed to be just about everything, wasn't anything to worry about.

'Yes, Mr Kingsley?' she prompted, finding his unusual silence unnerving, 'I'd like to get away as soon as possible, if you don't mind . . .'

'Why?'

She frowned, until she realised that he wouldn't know. 'I have a long way to walk,' she replied carefully.

'It's only eleven o'clock.'

'It gets dark early, though, and I'll have arrangements to make.'

He scanned her face and she saw him frown. 'Don't you have a car?'

'Not now.'

He turned to pace the length of the hall. At this rate, Christine thought desperately, she would be lucky to reach the other side of the loch before nightfall.

When he returned to her side, the green eyes narrowed and seemed to harden. She looked back at him coldly, with dislike. He was still frowning.

'Before I tackle those responsible,' he said, 'I'd like to know how you came to be here in the first place.'

He must mean those responsible for hiring her. She thought she had told him. 'It was probably my stepmother's fault,' she replied hesitantly. 'She must have given whoever was dealing with the matter the impression that I was older. If anyone had come to see the house, they would have soon discovered . . .'

'No one did,' he muttered abruptly. 'But a house is one thing; the hired help is quite another.'

She flushed with humiliation but she supposed that was exactly what she was. It was nothing to be ashamed of.

'Your employment with my firm,' he went on, 'is not what I was referring to, though I realise I should have made this clearer. How did you come to be living at Cragend before I bought it?'

'That's none of your business.'

'Miss Colwell!'

She lowered her eyes despairingly. She knew she had been rude but surely he had enough sensitivity to understand why she didn't want to go into that. 'Mr Kingsley,' she said tightly, 'as I'm leaving, does it matter?'

'I'd like to know.' He looked at her steadily and, to her surprise, added 'Please,' a little less curtly.

It held only a touch of friendliness but she felt it warm her and she couldn't resist it. 'My father bought Cragend nearly four years ago,' she began. 'Before that he lived and worked in London. He wanted to write—he was a very good writer,' she said quickly, as the green eyes glinted sceptically. 'Only he died before he became well known.'

'And you?'

'I left school and came with him, to look after him and do his typing. In London he'd always had a secretary, you see, and I was good at it.'

'Your stepmother?'

Must he know everything! 'She wasn't here to begin with. Dad met her on one of his trips to London. She never really settled . . .'

Mr Kingsley's mouth twisted. 'That, I suspect, is an understatement. So, why did your father choose to bury the two women in his life in the wilds of Scotland? People have been known to write successfully a little nearer civilisation.'

Christine's hackles rose and her chin flew up at his tone. 'I never considered myself buried alive, Mr Kingsley. The people around here are very friendly and the loch and mountains are wonderful. I love them.'

'Indeed?' The deep tone which somehow played on her nerves was dry with cynicism. 'How old are you, Miss Colwell?'

'Twenty-one.'

'And as soon as your father died, your stepmother took herself off.'

'She married again.'

'And sold the house and left you to fend for yourself.'

'I'm not a child, Mr Kingsley,' Christine exclaimed, resenting his harsh expression.

'Humm,' he murmured doubtfully. 'Have you really no one to turn to? If not a relative, perhaps an old family friend?'

'No,' she replied with weary patience. 'Now, if you don't mind, I should like to go.'

'I'm not finished yet,' he said sharply, with more than a hint of arrogance.

Christine's chin tilted again but she remained quite still. Obviously, if there was any dismissing to be done, it would be done by him.

'How easy is it to get staff in these parts?' he asked. 'Do you have anyone to help you?'

Which did he want answered first? 'I don't have any help,' she replied coolly. 'I've never needed any and, anyway, it would be difficult to find. People aren't keen to live in a place like this.'

'Only a moment ago you were telling me that you loved it.'

Her quick temper flared at his open derision. 'I'm telling you the truth, Mr Kingsley. The nearest house, other than old Jamie's, is easily ten miles away and Kinlagon is only a small village. The inhabitants there are too old to be of any use to you. You don't have to take my word for it, of course.'

'There's bound to be someone.' He shrugged, his

glance sweeping indifferently over the slender girl in front of him. 'Meanwhile, as you have been paid . . .'

'I haven't been paid anything!' she cried indignantly. 'At least, only once . . .'

'A roof over your head doesn't come cheap, nowadays. You can stay and look after me until I find someone else.'

Christine's heart sank as she stared at him uncertainly. It didn't seem important, who owed whom. An hour ago she had wanted to stay, now she wasn't so sure.

'It was you who told me to go,' she murmured evasively, while trying to think what to do.

'You are still under notice to go,' he retorted coldly. 'You're nothing like the kind of housekeeper I had in mind but I don't believe I'll have to put up with you for long.'

Odious man! He could have been nice about it at least! She would have liked to defy him to the bitter end but if she did, who would suffer but herself? She'd be a fool to turn down such an offer, insulting as it was. Even another week might give her time to find another job and somewhere to live.

'Thank you,' she murmured, lowering her thick lashes so that he wouldn't see the tears of despair in her eyes. 'I—I promise to do my best.'

'I'll see that you do, Miss Colwell.'

Christine swallowed. He didn't even have the generosity to sound grateful. He had asked questions but not because he was interested in her, personally. He had just made sure her background was relatively sound before keeping her on to look after his house and cook his dinner. That was all Mr Kingsley was interested in!

'If you'll excuse me, I'll get on then,' she muttered. 'Your bed will need making up.'

'I hope that a room is prepared for me,' he rapped. 'You haven't been entertaining your boyfriends in it?'

'The rooms have been ready all summer,' she replied

with a faint flush, hands clenched. She had never entertained a man in the sense he meant, in her life.

In the master-bedroom, she found sheets and quickly made up the bed. As she spread the down duvet, she glanced up to find Richard Kingsley standing in the doorway. She hoped he wasn't going to follow her around all the time, as if he doubted her ability to do anything properly.

Looking at him sharply, she said, 'I'm quite capable of doing a small job like this on my own.'

'So I see.'

'Mr Kingsley.' She paused, clutching a spare pillow and gazing at him over the top of it. 'Were you, I mean, are you sending me away because of the untidiness you found downstairs?'

'Among other things.'

He frowned, she could see he didn't care for having his motives questioned. 'I require someone more responsible. The untidiness wasn't important in itself, but it proves that you aren't completely reliable.'

'Just one small lapse?'

'You gave a party for your boyfriend.'

She clutched the pillow tighter. 'N—not exactly.'

'A wild party,' he continued remorselessly. 'He has just been on the telephone, asking if you were all right and saying how much he enjoyed it.'

'That would be Ken.' To her vexation she blushed. 'But he isn't my boyfriend.'

'Which makes it even worse,' he said severely. 'No one special and you put my house at his disposal.'

She sighed; it didn't seem worth arguing with Mr Kingsley once he had made up his mind. 'And the other things you have against me?'

'Not against you,' he retorted with grim patience. 'That I consider you too young and unsuitable for this particular job isn't necessarily a black mark against your character.'

'You call twenty-one, nearly twenty-two, too young?'

'I have my reasons for wanting someone older.'

'What if I'd pretended to be thirty?'

'I have eyes, Miss Colwell.'

To her surprise, he paled as he finished speaking and moved abruptly past her to the window. He looked like a man who had just been reminded of something unpleasant. Christine gazed at his broad back then uncertainly around the room, but she still couldn't see anything which might have been responsible for bringing such a look of unconscious despair to his face. She bit her lip sharply, not knowing what to make of him.

CHAPTER TWO

'THE view is magnificent,' Christine said softly, going up to him, always instinctively wishing to comfort where she sensed hurt. 'I'm sure you'll enjoy it.'

Turning back to her, he exclaimed almost savagely, 'While I am here, Miss Colwell, I advise you to keep such comments to yourself!'

'I—I'm sorry,' she stammered, feeling the hand which shot out to steady her as he nearly knocked her over; gripping so tightly that a tremor went through her. 'It was only a casual remark.'

As he released her, she returned to the bed. He didn't apologise for his roughness but continued to survey her moodily.

'Was this your father's room?'

'Yes.'

'He died here?'

After six months she was able to speak of it evenly. 'He died in Perth; a heart attack, and Leila wouldn't bring him home.'

'Your stepmother?'

Christine nodded.

'I see.'

He couldn't possibly but she let it pass. 'I can make up the bed next door, if you wish?'

'No, this will do for now.'

He moved away from her restlessly. 'What time is lunch?'

Lunch? She hesitated awkwardly, her cheeks pink. 'I thought I'd told you; there's no food . . .'

'Your friends ate it all last night?'

'They brought their own.'

'You managed all right for breakfast,' he pointed out.

'That was all I had.' She wondered if he was amusing

himself going over all this again. 'I keep poultry so I have eggs. Old Jamie, along the loch, gives me bacon and sometimes I buy milk.'

'Why didn't you apply for unemployment benefit?'

'Because I thought I was employed!'

He didn't speak for a moment, then he shrugged. 'Well, there's nothing that can't be sorted out. Meanwhile, if I give you some money, are you capable of buying some supplies?'

'Of course,' she retorted. 'But I couldn't get back in time for lunch.'

'Why not?' he snapped.

'Because, as I've already explained,' she said tersely, 'it's over ten miles to the nearest shop and I have to walk.'

'Can't you drive?'

'Yes,' she admitted, 'but I don't have a car.'

'Take mine.'

'Yours?'

'It won't bite,' he assured her sarcastically.

Christine drove as if it might. She found the high-powered sports car exciting but she was sure it had never been designed for twisting Highland roads. She was shown how to drive it with impatient precision, then dispatched to Kinlagon clutching a handful of notes.

As she drove back, mission completed, she was able to relax sufficiently to ponder over the car's owner. He would be somewhere in his middle thirties, she guessed. He might be older but she didn't think so. She recognised the lines of executive strain on his face. She supposed that he was good-looking, if one liked steely green eyes and strong, sensual features. The vitality in his face seemed strangely at odds with a certain tiredness but she had no doubt that, tired or otherwise, he was a force to be reckoned with. A wealthy one, too, she suspected. He had handed her a hundred pounds, as though it was ten pence and the car that she was driving must be worth a fortune!

None of which supplied the answer as to why he was here. For a few disturbing moments, until she had seen his passport, she had wondered if he could be an impostor. There could be no doubt of his identity and his firm had rung to say he was coming—she just wondered how he intended filling his days. Her father had told her that tycoons were usually workaholics, men who never stopped because they had to find something to use up their extraordinary amount of energy and satisfy their passion for work. Somehow she couldn't believe that Richard Kingsley had come to Cragend to pass a few relaxing weeks.

She heard him on the telephone in the study, as she staggered in with a heavy box of provisions. The people at the shop had been surprised that she had bought so much until she had explained. She hadn't told them that there was only one guest—they would find out soon enough, but by that time, some of Mr Kingsley's friends might have joined him and she would be gone anyway.

'Got everything?' He wandered into the kitchen as she was busy packing things away.

'The village store isn't Harrods, Mr Kingsley,' she replied drily. 'I've done my best. There's the receipted bill and your change.' She indicated where it lay on the table.

'You'd better hang on to it,' he acknowledged carelessly. 'I hardly think we'll manage on that for very long.'

How long did he intend staying? She glanced at him quickly, finding no answer in his impassive face. 'I'd prefer to ask for money as I need it, rather than leave it lying around.'

'You aren't suggesting that we have thieves, Miss Colwell?'

'Not like mice.' She couldn't help smiling; then, to hide her amusement, which she was sure he didn't appreciate, she added sharply, 'If anything should disappear, you would hold me responsible and I couldn't repay you. Occasionally we get strangers in the woods who could take something and be away in minutes without anyone seeing them.'

He picked up the change indifferently and put it into his pocket but ignored the bill. 'Have you thought about lunch yet?' he asked. 'Your Scottish air seems to have given me an appetite.'

'What do you usually have?' she countered uncertainly.

'Sandwiches and coffee in the office, when I don't go out.' He shrugged.

She could guess the kind of restaurants he frequented when he did. She didn't ask about the menus there. 'I can manage that and some soup,' she said, remembering that she had made some yesterday.

'I'd be obliged if you would bring it into the study,' he nodded. 'By the way, it's rather cool in there. I understood that there was central heating?'

'Dad was thinking of putting it in; Leila felt the cold badly. Surely,' Christine hesitated and flushed, 'she didn't imply it was in already?'

'I gather she did.' He smiled wryly. 'But don't worry, it's our fault for not checking.'

Christine tried not to but felt disgusted by Leila's dishonesty, which must have considerably added to the price she had received for the house. 'There's an electric fire upstairs somewhere,' she said weakly. 'I can fetch that.'

'It will do,' he agreed, leaving her abruptly.

He appeared to enjoy his lunch as much as he had his breakfast, but there was a kind of intense restlessness about him which puzzled her. Several times during the afternoon she saw him walking outside as if he couldn't settle to anything. Once, when she peeped through an upstairs window, frankly curious to see what he was doing, she saw him pausing every now and then as he wandered through the gardens in the direction of the loch. As she followed his tall figure, noting the breadth of his shoulders, the tautness of his legs beneath the black trousers, something stirred through her darkly, though she had no idea what it was.

She decided against returning Ken's 'phone call. He would understand that with Richard Kingsley here, the telephone was no longer hers to use freely. She would see him the next time she was in Inverness. Ken's grandparents used to live at Cragend, which was how she had met him. He had stopped by one day, introduced himself and offered to show her and her father around the district. Christine hadn't thought must about their friendship; she only knew that she liked going out with him occasionally.

Richard Kingsley went out again after dinner and it was dark when he returned.

'I thought you were lost!' Christine exclaimed, having begun to get anxious.

'Worrying about me, were you, Christine?' he asked cynically.

She was startled when he spoke her name but she liked it better than Miss Colwell. 'The paths around the loch can be dangerous,' she replied tightly, not knowing how to explain the feeling of dread which had come over her. 'You could easily fall and break a leg.'

'I realise that,' he said curtly, looking down at her with his glinting green eyes.

'You should get used to the countryside in daylight first,' she said crossly.

'That's just where you're wrong,' he muttered enigmatically, almost to himself. 'You must be familiar with the forests, Christine. Tomorrow you can show me around. I like company.'

That was what he had said before dinner when he had asked her to eat with him in the dining-room. She had tried to refuse but he had insisted, yet for all the notice he had taken of her she might never have been there. He had ignored her throughout the meal, concentrating instead on sheaves of closely typed papers which he had extracted in an ever-increasing stream from a bulging briefcase. His total absorption might have given her another chance to study him surreptitiously but had brought her no nearer to discovering anything more about him.

The days passed without her curiosity being satisfied. She was still wondering about him over a week later, as she took his morning coffee to the study. He was on the telephone; she could hear his raised voice as she crossed the hall. The telephone rang continually, until she was heartily sick of it. When he was out, she took calls from all over the world. If she hadn't discovered anything else, she was learning a great deal about his business and she knew enough to feel convinced that whatever his reason for being here, it was certainly not for a holiday.

The crash of the receiver made her wince but she grasped the opportunity to knock on the door and walk in. He waved to her to put down the tray, without looking up from what he was doing.

She watched him scribbling more of his never-ending notes and drew a deep breath. She had just received a letter from Ken, asking if she would go with him to a concert the following evening, and she wanted to make sure that it would be all right. 'Mr Kingsley . . .?'

'Yes?' He glanced up at her quickly.

Christine found her courage wavering. Didn't he know the meaning of patience? Meeting the pair of cold green eyes, she wondered what it would take to warm them. He had been much friendlier lately but there was always a discouraging chill about him.

'Could I have tomorrow night off, Mr Kingsley?'

'Why?'

Did he have to glower, as if she was asking for the impossible. She wasn't particularly keen to see Ken again but it had suddenly occurred to her that he might be able to help her to find a job.

'Someone has asked me out.'

'Who?'

She flushed. Did he have to treat her as her father had when she was seventeen! 'The—the friend who . . .'

'Nearly wrecked my house?' Up came a hand. 'You don't mean to say that you've forgiven him, Christine? He may have supplied the refreshments but he left you to do the clearing up.'

'He offered,' she said indignantly.

'It would have been more to his credit if he had done something.'

'Mr Kingsley.' Christine's blue eyes were defiant as she looked straight at him. 'You asked me to stay on until you got someone else. Could you give me a clearer idea as to how long you will require my services?'

His mouth twitched but just as she was trying to decide if he was laughing at her, he hauled himself to his feet and said abruptly. 'Why don't we take a walk by the loch and discuss the situation? I suppose I could do with a breath of fresh air.'

Christine had plenty to do but she nodded. As always when she was angry with him, something strangely vulnerable about him tugged at her heart strings.

Outside, he watched her face as she smiled at the antics of two crows chasing a sparrow hawk from a nearby clump of bushes. The wind was cold, with more than a hint of winter in it.

'You'd better button up your coat,' he advised. 'Do you get much snow here in winter?'

'Sometimes.' She smiled again.

'Why does the thought of snow please you?' He shot her a puzzled glance.

'Oh, I don't know.' She paused to consider. 'I suppose it's the thought of long cosy evenings in front of log fires. I feel ashamed of enjoying it, though, when I think of what the animals and birds have to suffer.'

'You're a funny girl,' he mused, catching her arm and drawing her on again. 'Someone of your age should be enjoying something entirely different.' The warmth in his eyes cooled. 'This boyfriend of yours, do you see much of him?'

Ken wasn't her boyfriend, not in the way Richard Kingsley meant, but she had tried to tell him this before, 'Ken lives in Inverness, so it's not very convenient.'

'Is he your lover?'

'No!' She flushed scarlet.

He merely shrugged, as if it didn't interest him much, one way or another. 'You may have tomorrow evening off,' he said condescendingly. 'But if you do go out, I don't want you back late.'

'I'm never back late, Mr Kingsley, but surely if I'm here in the morning, that's all that matters?'

She hadn't meant to goad him but sometimes his superior tones needled her. He usually set her down sharply when she spoke to him disrespectfully, but when he caught her other arm and swung her around to him roughly, she felt startled.

'While you are employed by me, Miss Colwell,' he glared, 'you will do as you're told. I'm the one who's paying your wages and I need you. I have to have someone who's around all the time and who is reliable.'

'You said I wasn't,' she reminded him.

'Maybe I've changed my mind,' he said tersely, letting go of her and turning moodily towards the loch. As Christine stumbled after him, he slackened his pace until she caught up with him, then asked: 'I found a boat yesterday. Does it belong to Cragend?'

'Yes.' She had thought that he had known about it. 'My father and I used to love going out in it.'

'So you didn't work all the time?'

'We usually went late at night,' she replied stiffly, retreating, as she usually did from his sarcasm.

'I don't fish,' he said curtly, as if there had to be a reason for doing something.

'Neither did he,' Christine explained patiently. 'He found the water soothing.'

'I might try it one day,' he murmured absently.

They walked a long way along the side of the loch and through the woods. He seemed to have forgotten he had only come out for a few minutes. He appeared to be extremely interested in everything about them. If

Christine hadn't known that such an idea was crazy, she would have sworn that he was trying to memorise every step he took.

'I hadn't realised that the ground around the house was so rugged,' he said, as they paused for a short rest.

'This is Scotland,' she retorted drily. 'But didn't you check?'

'Usually I check everything.' He frowned. 'Almost everything I've found here proves that it pays to.'

Christine was conscious of a tremor of disappointment. 'Do you mean,' she hesitated, 'that you've changed your mind about staying here?'

'No,' he replied curtly, walking on. 'It's exactly what I want. It will serve my purpose admirably.'

What purpose? she wondered anxiously, as she followed him but she dared not ask.

The next evening when he was in his room, the telephone rang. As she was ready to go out, just waiting for Ken to arrive, she hurried to the study to answer it. It was a woman. The voice which asked for Mr Kingsley was husky and attractive.

'I'll get him,' Christine said politely, a peculiar feeling in her stomach as she wondered who the woman was. Realising she was beginning to wonder too much about her brusque employer, she hurried upstairs.

It didn't help to steady her uneven pulses when he opened his bedroom door to her knock with only a towel wrapped around his waist. That he obviously didn't share her embarrassment seemed to indicate that he was used to women seeing him half naked.

Christine gulped, hastily averting her eyes. 'There's someone on the phone for you, Mr Kingsley. A lady.'

He nodded as if he wasn't greatly surprised, then said softly, 'Christine?'

'Yes?' Her eyes flew to his face.

'The name's Richard. I'm getting heartily sick of being called Mr Kingsley.'

'I'm your housekeeper!' she protested; such a

scandalised expression on her face that he grinned as he strode past her.

'All the more reason why you should obey me,' he threatened.

She had thought that he would put on a robe but he went downstairs exactly as he was. Christine followed, her eyes glued to the bareness of his broad back, no matter how hard she tried to look away. The arrogant strength of his head and shoulders made her shiver, while the hard, pronounced curve of his thighs beneath the towel shocked her somewhat. And she noticed that his long legs were shadowed by the same dark hair that covered his chest.

She didn't realise that she was so absorbed, until he closed the study door in her face, bringing her up to a sharp realisation of what she was doing. Flushing scarlet as she heard Ken's car in the drive, she rushed out to meet him. Her thoughts were confused but she knew instinctively that Ken musn't come into the house and find Richard Kingsley with only a towel around his waist. Ken prided himself on being broad-minded but she could imagine the way his eyebrows would rise if he came in here and found her boss wandering about half naked.

The concert was very enjoyable but late in finishing so that it was after midnight when they arrived back at Cragend.

'I'm sorry I've not been much help about a job,' Ken said as he wished her good night. 'If I hear of anything, I'll give you a ring but don't leave Cragend without letting me know.'

Watching his tail-lights disappearing along the drive, Christine bit her bottom lip with a sigh. Ken's father owned a big business in Inverness and she had hoped there might be something for her there but apparently he was laying people off and making others redundant.

Anxious, for fear Ken's rather noisy departure had disturbed Mr Kingsley, she crept quietly indoors. She almost dropped with shock when the lights were suddenly switched on to reveal him standing only few feet away.

'W-what on earth are you doing?' she exclaimed, when she found her voice.

'Walking around in the dark,' he snapped, as if it was the most natural thing in the world. 'Waiting for you to come home. I warned you not to be late, Christine.' His green eyes went scornfully over her. 'I suppose you've been necking by the lake?'

'Loch,' she corrected automatically, through indignant lips. 'We never stopped all the way home. The concert finished later than Ken thought it would . . .'

'A likely story,' he sneered. Christine could see that he was in a thoroughly bad mood. 'Don't you have a better excuse?'

She tried to ignore him. If she didn't they might soon be at each other's throats. 'Can I get you anything to eat before I go upstairs?' she offered with cool dignity.

'No thanks, I've had a drink.' Christine fancied he'd had a few. 'Run along.' He glared. 'I'll talk to you in the morning.'

She nodded, all of a sudden anxious to get away from him, and, because she hurried, forgot about the ragged places in the carpet. Before she knew what was happening, she had pitched forward and, like the previous time, he caught her.

Breathlessly she stared down at the strong, remorseless fingers gripping her arms and this time it was her heart that tripped.

'Let me go,' she whispered as his grip tightened, instead of releasing her.

'Don't you ever watch where you're going?' he murmured softly.

She didn't look at him; she didn't dare. Instead, unable to move, she fixed her eyes on where his dressing-gown parted over the breadth of his chest. She could see his shoulders, smooth-skinned and muscular. Her mouth was suddenly dry.

She heard the hiss of his indrawn breath and his eyes

darkened as one of his hands lifted to touch her cheek, then moved slowly to the delicate line of her jaw, gently touching her skin, tracing the fragile lines of the bones in her small face.

Christine wanted to pull away but she couldn't. Her whole body was achingly aware of the scorching touch of his fingers. She was more frightened of her own reactions than of him, though.

'Richard, please . . .'

She was stopped by his mouth as it crushed hers with a hunger that overwhelmed them both. She had never imagined the touch of his lips but if she had, it would have been nothing compared with the reality. She had been kissed before but never found it exciting. Being kissed by Richard Kingsley was an entirely new experience.

She hadn't known there could be so much intoxication in a mere kiss. That the world would stop, her heart would spin and stars would beat against her closed eyelids. She hadn't known that lips could be sweet as well as warm, possessing a magic that tugged at her senses, inviting her to drown in the enchantment of his arms. She clung to him as he enclosed her tightly in his arms and his mouth urgently explored hers.

Warning bells rang in her ears as he lifted her in his arms and began carrying her upstairs. She was clinging to him, wanting the magic to go on but not daring to think where it might end.

'Where are you going?' she managed to whisper, scarcely able to articulate through the wild beat of her heart.

'Where do you think?' he muttered, brushing feather-like kisses over her cheeks.

She looked into his hard-boned face and began to tremble. 'Please, Richard,' she begged, 'put me down.'

His mouth settled on hers gently and she had to fight against the weapons she sensed he was using. It wasn't easy. He scarcely had to touch her to have her senses reeling and she realised he probably knew it.

Mortification played its part in filling her with alarm. 'Please!' she whispered, beginning to struggle.

They were upstairs now and though he looked puzzled he let her slip from his arms.

'What's the matter, Christine?' he asked gently.

'This—just about everything!' she cried incoherently, suddenly rushing away from him along the corridor, into her room. Flinging herself on to her bed, she buried her face in her hands with equal abandonment, choking back sobs as she realised how she had behaved with a man who was almost a stranger.

She had crashed the door shut behind her but not locked it. That she instinctively trusted Richard not to come after her seemed to mock the anger she had managed to whip up against him.

Next morning after she had dressed, she ran quickly downstairs, but there was no sign of him. She guessed that he was outside and was dismayed to find herself trembling as she went into the kitchen. By the time he came in she felt more composed, and when he ate his breakfast as though nothing had happened, she was relieved. For him, a few kisses wouldn't be worth remembering. She wished she could feel as indifferent but at least he wasn't taunting her with them.

When he had finished eating, he asked her to go into the study. Christine followed him willingly enough. Last night he had said that he wanted to speak to her and this morning she wanted to speak to him.

As soon as he was sitting behind what she still thought of as her father's desk, she decided to get her say in first. It might even cancel what he had to say and save him the trouble.

'Mr Kingsley—Richard,' she amended to his fiercely drawn brows, 'I know I more or less agreed to stay until you found someone else but I'd like to leave straight away, if you don't mind. I'd appreciate it if you would pay me—just for the time you've been here will do. It doesn't matter about the rest.'

His brows re-shaped themselves in an upwards angle

with a hint of aloofness. 'I'm afraid I've changed my mind about replacing you, Christine. I was too hasty when I arrived. Since then I've had time to observe you and to think and I've decided, as I believe I've already hinted, that you will suit my purpose admirably.'

'What purpose?' She asked the question that she hadn't dared ask before.

'I'm not ready to reveal that yet.' The green eyes regarding her, darkened sombrely. 'You will learn in good time, but I will tell you that it's because you are familiar with the house and countryside and not because I fancy you in bed.'

'I . . .' She felt her cheeks flame but she went on doggedly, 'I realise that, Richard, but don't you see, the two of us being here alone is bound to cause talk. When I agreed to be housekeeper at Cragend, I expected to be looking after several people, not just one.'

He looked at her grimly. 'I'm going to London, Christine, and I'll be bringing back some friends, one of whom,' he hesitated, 'happens to be my fiancée.'

'Y-your fiancée?'

He didn't appear to notice the dismay she couldn't hide. 'Does that salve your conscience?'

Christine wasn't sure about her conscience but the rest of her felt chilled. 'Will your fiancée be staying long?'

'A few days perhaps.' He shrugged. 'She's a freelance model. I'm not sure what her commitments are.'

Surely to Richard first? Christine frowned. 'Was she the woman who rang last night?'

He nodded but didn't elaborate, leaving Christine to work out for herself whether it was his fiancée who had summoned him to London or if he had been going anyway.

'I'm still not sure,' she murmured doubtfully.

His mouth tightened, then he said curtly. 'If I offered you twice as much as I'm already paying you, for looking after me for perhaps two or three months, with a good bonus at the end of it, would that help you to make up your mind?'

It wasn't a case of money so much as getting away from him, yet how could she explain? She wasn't even sure that she could. She gazed at him mutely, her wide blue eyes reflecting her uncertainty. If he had a fiancée, surely there couldn't be a repeat of last night?

As if he had read her mind, Richard said smoothly, 'I was slightly drunk last night, Christine, but I don't make a habit of it. You have my word that what happened when you came in won't happen again.'

'I thought it was something like that,' she murmured distractedly. 'However . . .'

'Christine!' His eyes bored into her insistently. 'I need you so much, I can't let you go. If you leave, there are penalties I can impose. I could see to it that no one else would employ you.'

'You wouldn't . . .!'

'I might.' He steeled himself against the hurt in her eyes. 'It's not just a matter of looking after me,' he said quickly. 'Someone has to be here while I'm gone. I've arranged for a new carpet to be laid in the hall, before someone breaks their neck, and there's a load of stuff coming for the deep-freeze. There are also rooms to be prepared for my guests and the house tidied up generally.'

'All right,' she muttered sullenly, despising herself for giving in so easily yet knowing when she was beaten.

He had saved her pride by accepting that she was going to stay, without making an issue of it, but as he got to his feet he said sternly, 'I don't particularly care for you being here alone, Christine, but I don't want your boyfriend keeping you company. If I discover he has been here when I come back, you won't like what I'll have to say.'

Christine never knew how she passed the next few days. Before Richard had arrived she had been content enough but now, when she was on her own, there seemed to be a peculiar vacuum in her life. She was kept busy. A firm from Inverness arrived and fitted the carpet, a tough, self-patterned one that looked very nice, though Christine would have preferred rugs. Another firm brought the frozen food and, after packing it away, she began to thoroughly clean the house. It was quite a big job but she was grateful for the extra activity which tired her out and stopped her from thinking too much.

The rooms were dusty, rather than dirty. She hadn't actually neglected them but had devoted herself more to the garden and chopping wood for winter. Richard had restocked with coke and coal but before he had arrived she had anticipated having to burn logs all winter and had hauled as much firewood as she could from the forests.

She didn't get in touch with Ken but he rang her one evening. It was unfortunate that Richard should have chosen the same time to try and get through to her from London and had to wait until she stopped speaking to Ken. She'd had to endure a long lecture from him about using his telephone and time indiscriminately, which had annoyed Christine so much that she had crashed the receiver down recklessly before he had finished. When he rang straight back, with a matching fury, she had managed an apology but had seethed indignantly afterwards because he had so determinedly misjudged her. She wished she had accepted Ken's invitation to go out with him again instead of pretending that Richard was still there and that she was too busy.

Richard and his fiancée and another guest flew into Aberdeen airport and motored the rest of the way from there. When they arrived, Christine thought Richard looked tired. He wasn't driving the car himself. Another man got out of the driving seat as she ran impulsively to meet them.

'C-can I help to carry anything?' she stammered, as a tall, slender woman, standing beside Richard, raised haughty eyebrows at her breathless haste and she had to think of something to excuse her rather undignified behaviour.

'Who is this, Richard?' the woman asked as no one answered Christine's question.

'Christine Colwell.' Richard looked at Christine so closely that she wondered if she had a smut on her nose. 'She will be looking after us.'

As his glance progressed down her body she thought indignantly that if he had let her know he was coming, she could have been wearing something other than a pair of old jeans. She pressed her palms on her hips anxiously, unconsciously smoothing out creases, which sharpened the expression on the woman's face as Richard's eyes followed the movement of her hands unerringly.

He introduced them absently; the woman as his fiancée, Pearl Kristol, the man with them, Harry Skalka. Harry Skalka shook hands but Pearl merely nodded coolly, looking wholly disapproving.

'Couldn't you have found someone older?' Christine heard her saying to Richard as they went inside.

'I need someone with plenty of energy—and intelligence,' he replied.

Christine knew she wasn't supposed to be listening but she didn't care. If Richard needed someone—for anything, why didn't Pearl volunteer? Richard had mentioned two or three months and if Pearl worked freelance, she must be able to spare that amount of time from her career. Perhaps not? Christine was ashamed to find herself answering her own question cattily. Miss Kristol was beautiful and sophisticated but she must be getting on for thirty, which was old for modelling.

In the hall, Richard spoke to her curtly. 'You'd better take Pearl to her room, Christine, then start dinner. I realise I should have let you know we were coming but there are only three of us.'

Harry Skalka, a tall man in his thirties with a pleasant face, smiled at her. 'If you require any help just shout, Christine. I'm better than either of these two in the kitchen.'

Pearl followed Christine upstairs and failed to look impressed by the amount of polishing and scrubbing that had been done in the room she was shown into.

'By the way,' she said coldly, as Christine turned to leave her, 'I'm Mrs Kristol, not Miss. Mr Kingsley forgot to mention it.'

So Richard's fiancée was a widow, or she could be divorced. Downstairs again, Christine was aware that Pearl didn't care two hoots whether anyone knew she'd been married or not. She had just been making sure that no housekeeper was going to use her Christian name. Pearl was beautiful but cold, without an obvious sense of humour. Pausing in the kitchen, before she started cooking, Christine wondered why she felt so antagonistic. No matter how cold and unfriendly Mrs Kristol was, it was none of her business. She couldn't understand how actually seeing Richard with his fiancée should suddenly seem like having a bad dream turn into a nightmare.

CHAPTER THREE

CHRISTINE managed to produce an appetising meal of steaks, French fries and her own vegetables from the garden. Pearl complained that fried potatoes were fattening and ate mostly lettuce but the two men appeared to enjoy everything.

Richard had wanted Christine to have dinner with them in the dining-room. When she had refused, he had become quite annoyed with her in front of Pearl and Harry but she had stuck to her guns. Pearl might be a—no, she wouldn't say it, for she could be mistaken and even if she wasn't, it wasn't very lady-like, but surely Richard could have used a little tact and not looked so put out in front of her, simply because his hired help refused to dine with him.

The following day he retreated into his study again, spending long hours there, despite Pearl's constant protests that she was being neglected. When he wasn't working, Christine was sometimes startled to find him standing behind her, watching her. She wasn't sure that he was fully aware of what he was doing on these occasions. He was more likely to be sorting out some problem in his mind than to be interested in what she was doing, but it was doubtful that Pearl understood this. Once, when she had come across them unexpectedly, she had stared at Christine very suspiciously.

Christine frequently heard her railing at him about her unsuitability as a housekeeper—and just about everything else as far as Christine could make out! She had even heard her say that the plainest ones were always the worst.

'Do you think I notice how she looks?' Richard had snapped.

Obviously he hadn't realised he had been overheard

but Christine had flushed with humiliation. If she had needed proof that when he looked at her he seldom saw her, he provided it in that one terse sentence. She tried to tell herself, drily, that it was just as well he didn't notice her, as she was usually enveloped in mop-caps and dusters, but, nevertheless, to hear him put it in words, hurt.

She discovered that Harry Skalka was an American doctor and that he was Richard's cousin, but precious little else. She liked him, he was fun to have around, in a nice kind of way. He made his bed and didn't mind washing dishes and brushing floors and he usually walked with her around the loch each afternoon, to old Jamie's, to help to carry the extra milk.

Sometimes the weight of Pearl's disapproval grew too much for her and she was glad of a chance to escape. The weather was getting cold for the garden, though she managed to get the vegetable patch turned over, ready for the spring. Harry had helped her but Richard had spoiled it all by discovering them at it and asking derisively, that as they would all be gone by spring, who was going to reap the benefit? Strangely, Harry hadn't retaliated, it was Christine who had put her spade down and walked mutinously away. She wished she could have followed Harry's example and taken no notice but if she had stayed she might have lost her temper and said things she would have regretted later.

As she and Harry returned from Jamie's one day, she ventured in a rather strained voice, 'Sometimes I can't seem very well trained when I get angry with my employer. Maybe I don't actually say much but I know you've noticed how I feel.'

Harry smiled as he slanted her a sideways look. 'You're exactly what he needs. You have the right kind of patience, the kind that isn't so unending that he feels he can walk right over you. Humour him, Christine; he will need it, but don't be tempted to always give in to him.'

He seemed about to say more, then he changed his

mind and she still didn't feel she knew him well enough to ask too many questions about Richard. Maybe she was more frightened than reticent? It might be cowardly but she couldn't face the possibility of being told that he had something terribly wrong with him. She clung to her ignorance, finding it easier to bear.

'Mrs Kristol has been married before,' she murmured tentatively, finding her curiosity over Pearl even harder to restrain, if for different reasons. She tried to pretend that she was showing a detached interest in Richard's fiancée, while living in daily dread that he wouldn't be happy with her.

'Yes,' Harry replied, not so gently this time. 'She was married to one of Richard's best friends—Ben was killed when they were all in New York together. In a way, Ric blames himself. Ben wasn't keen to do a job, he thought he couldn't manage it, but Richard gave him no alternative.'

'Was it something illegal?'

'No, of course not!' Harry looked sternly at her paling face. 'Ric's one hundred per cent straight in all his dealings, but Ben had an expensive wife and not enough confidence to earn the kind of money she was always demanding. He was always asking Ric for more responsibility but he didn't have the ability. Pearl, for all she was continually pushing him, reckoned afterwards that he had been so upset, he probably never saw the truck he crashed into.'

Christine clenched her hands. 'Richard felt responsible?'

'She saw to it that he did. Richard's a far bigger fish than Ben ever was, or could have been.'

Harry broke off, as if he knew he had said too much, but he sounded bitter. They walked in silence for a while, with the water of the loch lapping at their feet, while Christine tried to digest what he had told her. Surely Richard hadn't allowed a guilty conscience to force him into asking Pearl to marry him? But he wouldn't be the first man to have fallen into such a trap. The cold wind blowing from the mountains seemed to touch her heart and she silently berated herself for thinking nonsense.

As a cloud covered the sun, giving the loch and hills a greyish cast, Harry turned to her and asked abruptly, 'What's a lovely young girl like you doing here? Richard tells me you come from London.'

She nodded, faintly amused by his description of her. 'He probably told you enough to save me going over it again, at least the reason why I came here?' When he nodded, she added wryly, 'I like London and I like living at Cragend, I suppose because I'm basically contented and adaptable. For years I was at boarding school and I liked that, too.'

'Haven't you considered a proper career?'

She wondered why he didn't take what she was doing now seriously. 'I could take a domestic science course and become a professional housekeeper,' she pointed out. 'Or I could be a secretary—I've had some experience. Or even a nurse. Nursing has always appealed to me but I think I'd be too inclined to weep over my patients. Anyway,' she said, thinking of Richard, 'I'm going to have time to decide what to do—before I commit myself.'

'As long as you take a few months.' He smiled enigmatically.

Sometimes, after this conversation with Harry, Christine found herself watching Pearl and Richard more closely than she had ever done before. Richard allowed her to have her meals in the kitchen but he insisted that she joined them afterwards in the lounge for coffee. She was sure that if she had loved someone enough to get engaged to them, she would have been more starry-eyed than either Pearl or Richard appeared to be. They rarely sat together, or even exchanged loving glances, as she had supposed all lovers did. Had Pearl trapped him, as Harry had implied, or had Richard nursed a secret passion for her, long before she was widowed? Pearl was beautiful with such an amazingly slim figure that she made Christine hate her own, more pronounced curves, but she didn't know if they were lovers. Pearl had hinted that they were and Christine had no idea what went on after she went to bed. Perhaps it was just as well, she thought bleakly.

One evening, while Pearl and Richard were out in the car, Harry told her why Richard needed her. 'How much do you know about what he is suffering from?' he asked grimly.

'Very little,' she replied, the colour fading from her face. She was busy drying coffee cups and almost dropped one of them when she heard what Harry was saying.

'Look, honey,' he suggested gently, 'why not make us a cup of your nice English tea that I've got so fond of and let me explain?'

The kettle was already boiling on the old-fashioned kitchen range which now had an ample supply of coke. After making the tea, she carried it in the big, cosy-clad teapot to the table where Harry was waiting with biscuits and mugs. Sitting down beside him, she poured it out. Her hands wouldn't stop trembling but she was heedless of what he thought, she was too eager to hear what he had to say.

'About Richard?' she prompted, her blue eyes full of an urgency she wasn't aware of.

He seemed set upon going about it in a roundabout way. He didn't look at her as he concentrated on stirring his tea. 'My mother, Richard's aunt, married an American but our two families have always visited and Richard and I have always been close friends.'

'You must know all about him?' she whispered.

'A lot.' He smiled wryly. 'I don't suppose there's anyone who knows all about him.'

'I hardly know anything.'

Catching her wistful tone, Harry glanced at her sharply but only said, 'If Ric hides anything, it's himself. He has a brilliant brain but a man like him is always complex. He's never had things handed to him on a plate. He's had to burn the midnight oil and sometimes fight desperately all the way. Even when you reach the top today, you have to struggle to maintain your position.'

'I realise how hard he works.' Christine twisted her cup in her hands, 'You must have heard him in the study . . .'

Harry nodded and looked at her thoughtfully. 'Remember the other day I mentioned Pearl's husband being killed? Well, Richard was rushing her to the hospital, hoping they might be in time, when she suddenly threw a fit of hysterics and grabbed his arm. Fortunately, no one else was involved. They hit a concrete wall and Richard hit his head but they only appeared to be suffering from shock and were able to continue on to the hospital in a cab. He actually thought no more about the knock he had received until his eyes began playing him up and he started having severe headaches. However, repeated investigations in one of the best clinics in the States reveal nothing but severe eye strain . . .'

'Eye strain?' Christine was bewildered. 'Is that serious?'

'Not necessarily,' Harry replied soberly. 'Not if it is dealt with in time. In Ric's case, if he neglects it much longer, it could render him temporarily, even permanently, blind.'

Blind! Christine could scarcely imagine what this would mean to Richard and she gazed at Harry, undisguised horror in her eyes.

'Does blindness shock you that much?' He frowned.

'No—well.' She pulled herself together. 'No caring person could help being upset by it, because of its effect on the person involved. I don't find it repulsive, if that's what you mean. I just shudder to think what it would do to a man like Richard.'

'It isn't easy for anyone, however brave people appear to be,' Harry said soberly. 'But the whole world can lose out when someone like Richard goes blind. It may not come to that, though. His ophthalmologist over there, firmly believes that a complete rest for his eyes and from his business activities for a few weeks, should do the trick. Richard eventually agreed to it and I'm here to see that he doesn't change his mind.'

'Will you be staying at Cragend?'

'No. I'm working in London but I'll be in constant touch.'

Still in the throes of shock, Christine whispered, 'Wouldn't it be better for Richard to be in London with you?'

'Not at the moment,' Harry said firmly. 'He wouldn't agree to have the treatment there, anyway. This house had already been purchased and he decided to make use of it. He assured me that there was somone have to look after him but I had to come and see for myself.'

'If I was suitable?'

When he murmured ruefully, 'Forgive me,' she smiled. 'I don't mind, it was the sensible thing to do. I'm probably a fairly competent housekeeper but I've no nursing experience.'

'That's not important.' He looked at her keenly. 'Not everyone would have done, but I'm convinced that you are caring and compassionate enough to do the job admirably. You're also young enough to stand the strain. I'm totally satisfied he'll be in the best of hands. Of course, I've had a word with your local GP and I will be visiting and keeping in constant touch myself.'

'Wouldn't Pearl have been better . . .?'

'No,' he broke in curtly but he seemed reluctant to discuss her. 'It's better that she amuses herself in London and keeps out of his hair.'

Christine gazed at him doubtfully. What a funny remark to make about Richard's fiancée. Lowering her too-revealing eyes, she asked, 'When does he begin the actual treatment? He's already been here quite a while.'

'He wanted to get to know the terrain, make sure he was comfortable with it. When his eyes are bandaged so that he can't see, he has to be able to envisage his surroundings, Christine, otherwise he might feel he was going mad.'

Christine drew an unsteady breath. 'You think rest and time is all that's necessary?'

'We are hoping so,' Harry said gently. 'He's rather a unique case and he has been under close observation. He will continue to be but only time will actually prove if we are right.'

Christine swallowed an obstruction in her throat. 'W—when . . .?'

'Look,' Harry said quietly, 'Pearl and I are leaving for London tomorrow. Richard's following in a day or two. Why don't you come with him and I'll bring you both back?'

She was tempted but she didn't think Richard would want her. Then there was Pearl. It was her privilege to be at his side while she had the chance. Christine couldn't see her relinquishing her rightful place to the housekeeper, or to any other woman, come to that.

'I think I should stay here,' she murmured, as Harry waited for her reply.

He seemed about to argue, then he nodded reluctantly. 'It might be just as well. You'll have everything ready and be here to welcome him. There's nothing worse at the end of a longish journey than a cold, empty house.'

Christine thought about that after Pearl and Harry had departed the next morning. She wondered why Richard hadn't gone with them. When she had asked him, he had glared at her and said that he had no desire to spend three days hanging around London, unable to go to his office and having to endure the curiosity and condolences of his friends.

She must have looked doubtful, for he had added, 'There are things I want tidied up here, in the study, while I'm still permitted to use my eyes. Since you now apparently know what's wrong with me, I wonder why I should need to explain! Then there's a room to get ready downstairs.'

'Downstairs?'

'I don't intend to make a fool of myself by falling down the stairs,' he had snapped.

Christine sighed as she finished the breakfast dishes and went and knocked on the study door. When he looked anything but pleased at the interruption, she said firmly, 'You said I was to come and see you about the room as soon as I was finished in the kitchen. There's only one room on the ground floor which isn't used and that's the one around the corner at the end of the hall.'

'Okay.' He rose abruptly. 'Let's take a look. Then I can get used to it.'

'Why didn't you get your fiancée to help you?' Christine heard herself asking sharply.

He didn't even bother to answer and she guessed that she deserved his withering glance. Anyway, Pearl wouldn't have known where to begin. Her tongue was the only industrious thing about her. Christine winced at the lecture she had received from her before she had left—about girls who fell for their employers. She had warned Christine that if frustration and boredom drove Richard to make a pass at her, she shouldn't take him seriously.

'These kind of situations induce the old master and slave atmosphere,' she had said icily. 'He ought to have got someone older.'

To her shame, Christine had retorted furiously, 'Why can't you come and look after him yourself?'

'Because I have my career to think of,' Pearl had replied haughtily.

Perhaps fortunately, Christine thought scornfully and couldn't help exclaiming, 'I would have thought that Richard's health was more important than any career; especially,' she'd had to force herself to go on, 'when you're soon to be married.'

Pearl's eyes had been suddenly veiled with secrecy. 'We haven't actually fixed a date for our wedding yet.

Richard doesn't want to wait but it never pays to be too hasty.'

Christine would liked to have known what she meant. She suspected Pearl used every situation she found herself in to her own advantage as far as possible and that she never committed herself to anything about which she was doubtful. Had her ambiguous remark had anything to do with Richard's eyes? Surely Pearl couldn't be considering dropping him if he didn't make a complete recovery? Christine refused to believe that even Pearl could be that callous, but she knew that if she had loved a man with Richard's affliction, she would have wanted to marry him immediately, so that she could always be with him.

The room at the end of the hall had, in recent years, been used as a store-room and was full of old junk and very dusty. 'What was its purpose originally?' Richard asked moodily, surveying it from the doorway.

'I believe it was once a gun room,'Christine replied. 'It makes sense, when Cragend was built as a shooting lodge. At least, according to some old plans Dad found. There's a washroom through that door.'

'I'll only need a bed and a wardrobe, maybe somewhere for my socks,' Richard said indifferently. 'If I'm going to be blind for a few months, the less I have to fall over, the better.'

As Christine went pale, he looked at her mockingly. 'You ought to take a lesson from my fiancée. She doesn't burst into tears whenever I mention my eyes. She has more faith in my recovery.'

That's what you think! Christine thought, hating him. Her eyes were stinging but she refused to believe she was crying. No one with any sense would cry over a brute like him! She must have been crazy, last night, to have imagined she was beginning to care for him.

Turning her back, so that she could surreptitiously wipe away a shameful tear, she asked, with as much dignity as she could muster, 'Shall we bring your bed down from upstairs?'

'That won't be necessary,' he said tersely. 'I'll have a new bed delivered.'

'Won't that be a bit of a waste?' she demurred, 'when there are perfectly good ones upstairs?'

'All weighing a ton, by the looks of them,' he said drily as, once more composed, she turned around to look at him. 'Who's going to help me get one down? And don't say yourself,' he scoffed, as she opened her mouth. 'A fat lot of good you'd be to me with a broken back!'

'I was going to suggest asking Ken to give you a hand.'

'Ah, yes, lover boy,' he grated, the green eyes glinting. 'Well, thanks but no thanks. I'll order a new one and let that be the end of it, though I have no doubt that your Mr Granger is an expert when it comes to beds.'

She averted her head swiftly as tears threatened again. During the past week Richard hadn't been able to have a go at her because of his guests. They had shielded her, unwittingly, from his darker moods but now she seemed more vulnerable than ever.

It was only by ignoring most of his remarks that she was able to get through all the work she did. Richard helped her to carry most of the rubbish outside but though he came frequently to see how she was gettting on, he left her to do the rest herself. She was tired when he suggested a walk after tea but because he looked so pale and grim, she found herself giving in to him.

Obediently, she reached for her coat. 'It will probably do us both good.' She smiled ruefully. 'I feel like your room looked when we first started.'

He caught her hand as they walked through the woods. 'Practice for you,' he teased, tightening his hold as something like fire shot through her and she would have drawn back. 'You'll have to get used to leading me around when I return from London.'

She doubted if, when it came to it, he would submit to being led around but rather than risk destroying the sudden warmth between them, she said nothing. She liked the feel of his hands. They were well cared for but strong and well shaped and she sensed that with a woman he loved they could be tender.

Thinking of Pearl, she pulled away from him and ran to the lochside, as though seeking to escape Pearl in the grey, choppy water.

'We get wild geese in winter,' she said quickly. 'They come from Norway—you'll enjoy seeing them.'

'Hearing them, you mean,' he replied coldly, catching up with her.

Her eyes widened in dismay as she realised the mistake she had made. 'Oh, Richard, I'm sorry.' She laid a remorseful hand on his arm. 'That was clumsy of me . . .'

'You don't have to apologise!' he snapped.

'But I should—oh, please!' she pleaded, a tear she wasn't conscious of, falling on his hand. 'Please say you forgive me.'

Involuntarily he pulled her close, his arms clasping her tightly as he licked the tear from his hand. 'God, Christine,' he groaned, 'don't you understand? I don't want you to change, to grow into someone who thinks twice before she speaks and who guards every word. Everything's changing, I don't want you to. There's something so natural, so wholesome and generous about you. I feel like a prospector who's found gold, my darling.'

Christine looked up into his hard-boned face and murmured his name. Slowly, he bent his head, his glittering gaze fixed on her mouth and she closed her eyes as his lips descended gently on hers. She sighed as she felt what she now recognised as desire running through her veins. She trembled, her heart pounding, standing very still, fighting the dangerous feelings he evoked while yielding to the truth that she had been evading for days. She loved this man—there was no way she could deny it. She could only try to hide it.

'Christine?'

Her name was like music on his lips, which, when played back to her had an erotic effect on her senses. When the provocative brush of his mouth deepened into a bruising kiss, she was lost. Wanting him was a torment that might increase with every passing day and, though moments like this might be unwise, she wasn't strong enough to resist them.

The pressure of his mouth eased, becoming gentle again and more persuasive. His fingers trailed from her face to the beautiful swell of her breasts where he paused, his hand warm against her flesh, as if waiting for a small sign of encouragement.

Christine responded to his kiss, light-headed from the magic it evoked in her body, but his touch on her breast startled her. She sensed that he was asking for something but she was afraid of giving too much, too soon. She was torn between her love for him, which made her want to throw herself completely at his mercy, and a reluctance to be used by a man who loved another woman.

Yet her longing for him was so intense that she found it impossible to push him away. However, instead of taking immediate advantage of her obvious inability to fight him, Richard sighed thickly and rested his cheek against her hair. Keeping her in the curve of his arm, after a moment he tipped her chin up tenderly and kissed her lips lightly.

'Let's go home,' he murmured. 'It's warmer there.'

Without protest she stayed in the shelter of his arms as he guided her back along the path to the house. Words seemed unnecessary, the silence between them was warm and comfortable and neither of them wanted to break it. There was also a sharp current of awareness which had Christine holding her breath. It came as a rude awakening when no sooner had Richard closed and locked the front door than the telephone rang.

'Let it ring,' he muttered, 'it will stop.' Then when it didn't, 'Oh, hell, will you answer it, darling? Tell whoever it is that I'm out somewhere. I don't think I could talk to anyone just now.'

As she obeyed, Christine's heart sank. Was he frightened it was Pearl? Not even a man as adept as Richard at coping with every contingency, might have the nerve to speak to his fiancée after just kissing another girl.

Christine's hand shook with shared guilt as she lifted the receiver. To her relief it was Ken.

'Where have you been?' he asked. 'I've been trying to get you for ages.'

'Out—walking.'

'Alone?'

He sounded put out. 'No, with—Mr Kingsley.'

'Is that part of your duties?'

'Yes, at least,' she floundered. 'Listen, Ken, I'll explain when I see you. It's not easy on the phone.'

'How about coming out with me tonight?' he suggested, in more conciliatory tones. 'Just for a drink. We don't have to go anywhere special.'

Christine wondered if she could. The tension between Richard and herself made her tremble. She didn't understand it; it was probably just some trick of the night and their senses, but she felt that it might be safer to spend the rest of the evening with Ken.

'I think it will be all right.' She was about to say she would go and see, when the receiver was snatched rudely from her hands.

'Granger?' Richard barked, giving Ken a mere instant to acknowledge, 'Christine isn't free to make dates just now, she's far too busy.'

Christine couldn't hear Ken's reply but he must have asked for how long, for Richard snapped, 'Not for the next two or three months.'

The receiver was dropped into place with a crash. Christine stared at it, her eyes wide with distress, 'You had no business,' she began indignantly.

'Shut up,' Richard said violently. 'I'm sorry if you feel disappointed but while you are working for me I'm afraid you will have to stick to your duties.'

She looked at him mutinously. All the warm feeling had gone. He was white about the mouth with a temper she was sure wasn't justified. 'I have to have some time off.'

'Maybe after I get back from London and settle down,' he agreed grudgingly. 'Didn't Harry mention that I can't be here alone? He's told me often enough.'

She nodded dumbly.

What she considered an unreasonable anger, didn't abate. He prowled about the study like an enraged tiger. 'You'll have to get out of the habit of merely shaking or nodding your head when I speak to you. How the hell am I to know what you mean when I'm blind?'

'I'm sorry, Richard,' she retorted, getting a little angry herself. 'I'll try and remember, otherwise you'll just have to guess. But you won't be blind.'

'You have another name for it?' He fixed her with jeering green eyes.

'I'll admit that you won't be able to see for a while but there's a difference . . .'

'Oh, never mind,' he said curtly, running a suddenly weary hand around the back of his neck. 'We needn't argue the finer points, need we? Just go and see what you can find for dinner, there's a good girl. I think I stayed outside too long . . .'

They were back on their old footing with a vengeance but, instead of feeling resentful, Christine was grateful. Richard was cool and distant again and she wouldn't let herself imagine that something about him was begging for understanding. She was sensible enough to realise that for the next month or two she was going to be essential to him and anything that even remotely threatened to take her away from him was bound to cause panic. Even in a man who didn't normally know the meaning of the word.

After dinner, when he retired to the study, she found a book and went to bed. It was no penalty to go to bed early after the long day she'd had; if only her mind had been willing to come with her, instead of refusing to budge from the lone figure downstairs.

The following morning was fine, with the first frosts glinting in the glens, reflecting the beauty of the snow-capped mountains. Christine deserted her skirt in favour of jeans and a jumper which immediately felt warmer.

She was giving the old stray dog some breakfast by the back door when she turned to find Richard standing behind her.

'What's this?' he asked curtly.

Tossing her dark, tumbled curls from her small face, she glanced at him in dismay. 'He doesn't eat much but the weather's getting colder. Please don't send him away.'

'Who's going to?' he asked with terse impatience. 'Really, Christine, must you always think the worst of me? I presume he lived here before I came?'

She flushed at his assumption that the dog belonged to her and that she had simply turfed him out, believing that he wouldn't be welcome.

'He's a stray,' she said quickly. 'He only calls for a meal now and then. Sometimes, on cold nights, he condescends to sleep in the kitchen but I don't think anyone could really tame him.'

His face softened as he looked at her again. 'I don't mind you having him inside, Christine. A good brushing would do him no harm but a dog around the place isn't such a bad idea. I remember when I was a kid, I always wanted one. Perhaps—oh, well, never mind. What I came to ask, before I got diverted,' he said, 'was whether you would condescend to take me out for an hour? I know I spoke too sharply last night and that you're still feeling angry with me, but I'd really appreciate it if you would show me something of your countryside.'

'I thought Pearl did that?'

For once he didn't take exception to the sharpness of her tongue when she mentioned his fiancée. 'Yes, well, when Pearl gets behind a wheel the only place the car seems to want to go to is the nearest pub.'

Again Christine found her coat, beginning to realise what a full time job she had taken on. Harry had been right in maintaining it took someone young and fit to keep up with Richard. And when he smiled and looked repentant, she had about as much will-power as a pound of melted butter.

She drove the car carefully, wondering if Richard's real objective, this morning, was to see how competent she was. Somehow, she thought it would take more than the scenery to entice him from his beloved office.

'You're very good,' he said, as her confidence grew. 'You've been well taught.'

'I passed my test in London,' she told him. 'Just before we came here. Dad was never fond of driving so I got plenty of practice. That is, until Leila came and she took over, so it's getting on for two years since I was out much. Not that there was much time to go out.' She smiled ruefully. 'Dad kept to a fairly busy schedule.'

'Would you have gone on living with your father and his new wife?' he asked coolly. 'She must have felt very *de trop*.'

Having been buoyed up by his praise of her driving, such veiled criticism was like a douche of cold water. She flushed, and feeling his eyes taunting her hot face, was ashamed to find herself thinking that in another few days he wouldn't be able to see the tell-tale colour he seemed to enjoy bringing to her cheeks.

Leila had been another Pearl, reluctant to put even a foot inside a kitchen. Since there was plenty of evidence that this was the kind of woman Richard appreciated, Christine's soft lips set in stubborn silence. She might have told him that if Leila had shown the slightest tendency of being even reasonably domesticated she would probably have left Cragend very quickly to get on with a life of her own.

'I don't think Leila ever felt *de trop*,' she said at last, more revealingly than she had intended. 'She preferred having me there to type for Dad and look after the house so that she could go regularly to London.'

'Humm,' Richard murmured, then he appeared to lose interest in Leila. 'Look,' he said, as they rounded a bend with panoramic views, 'how about stopping somewhere for lunch? It will save you cooking and make a change.'

Christine sighed. Richard being nice again, was hard to resist. 'I'd love to.' She smiled, unable to hide her pleasure. 'I'm only in jeans though.'

'You look great,' he said, returning her grin, though his eyes held a less casual interest than his voice. In the days ahead, he would remember her slim and very feminine figure, the small face, the beautiful blue eyes with their sparkle of clear innocence, the mouth he always had an incredible urge to kiss.

Turning from her abruptly, he ordered her to drive to the nearest hotel.

CHAPTER FOUR

THEY lunched well. When Christine protested that it was too much in the middle of the day, Richard said they could have a light supper.

'Consider you are having a day off, or almost.' He smiled. 'I'm sure you deserve one.'

The hotel, once an ancestral castle, had been lovingly restored by a descendant of the same clan and carefully endowed with all the trappings of modern luxury. Mindful of her jeans, Christine would have driven straight on if Richard hadn't stopped her. She needn't have worried. No one took any notice of their casual dress though she suspected that they wouldn't have got away with it for dinner.

'I'd like to see you in a long, very feminine gown,' Richard startled her by musing as they went home. 'Wear one this evening.'

They were on dangerous ground again but Christine pretended to humour him. 'If I know you,' she laughed, 'you'll be so busy making up for lost time, you won't notice if I wear a sack. Anyway,' she made herself add deliberately, 'I couldn't compete with Mrs Kristol.'

'Perhaps not,' he agreed shortly. 'Forget about the dress. It was a crazy suggestion.'

Christine shivered, suddenly feeling chilled.

'Tomorrow,' he said, breaking the strained silence between them as they reached Cragend, 'I have a taxi coming to take me to the airport. I'll fly straight from there to London.'

'For how long?'

'I'm not sure how long I'll be away,' he said tersely. 'Two or three days, I should think, at the most.' He glanced at her quickly as they left the car. 'Harry said you refused to come with me.'

'I'm sure he didn't put it quite like that,' she replied awkwardly. 'He merely wondered if it might be a good idea and I said I thought I would be of more use staying here. In this weather,' she searched for a convincing excuse, 'a house left without a fire for two days can take as long to warm up.'

'I won't be an invalid,' he said drily. 'If you won't come, you won't, but I'd be happier having you with me than knowing you were here on your own.'

'I'm used to it.'

'I want you to promise you won't leave Cragend while I'm gone,' he insisted.

'Don't worry,' she replied. 'Just come back safe yourself, that's all that matters.' Then, frightened that she had revealed too much, she asked brightly, 'Will Mrs Kristol be meeting you in London?'

'I don't think so.' He looked at Christine narrowly, as if he knew, by her frequent references to Pearl, what she was doing. 'I believe she's abroad somewhere, on an assignment. She will be here for Christmas, though.'

What sort of a girl went off and left her fiancé to cope alone at a time like this? Christine knew that if she had been engaged to Richard, she could never have deserted him when he needed her most. Did Pearl deserve any consideration, Christine wondered, while not being quite sure what she meant.

Richard slaved in the study for the rest of the day, as she had suspected he would. She regretted the large lunch they'd had when he refused to have anything but coffee and a sandwich for dinner. At ten, when he was still taking calls from all over the world and showed no signs of flagging, she decided to go to bed.

He wandered into the lounge just as she was switching off the television. She hadn't been watching it but had put it on because she hadn't wanted him to guess that she had been sitting there thinking of him.

'Not going to bed already?' he asked.

'As a matter of fact I was,' she retorted, returning his taunting glance coolly. 'I hope the telly wasn't disturbing you. I know how busy you are and I kept it low.'

He laughed, immediately seeing through her. 'Why don't you come straight out and say it, Christine? You aren't always so reticent. You don't admire my industry, you're disapproving of it.'

Her blue eyes widened indignantly. 'I do admire how hard you work, I just wonder if you aren't doing too much?'

'Some think I'm not doing enough,' he retorted drily. 'Lately I've had reason to suspect that there are those who would soon lose interest in me if I lost the ability to make money.'

Christine frowned without paying much attention. 'You'll have to slow down when you come back . . .'

'How am I supposed to fill in the time?' Sticking his hands in his pockets, he crossed the room restlessly, pausing by the fire to stare at the still brightly burning logs. 'If I'm to be a kind of guinea-pig, it could pay off eventually, but it's not going to be easy.'

'Maybe you make things difficult for yourself?' she murmured.

He turned to her aggressively as she stood with her hands clasped before her, looking at him nervously. 'What, exactly, do you mean by that?'

Christine swallowed. 'Well, maybe any other person with your affliction might have been told to take a complete rest, but could anyone trust you to stick to such a course without making sure that you had no alternative?'

'It wasn't so much that others didn't trust me,' he snapped. 'I couldn't trust myself.'

'Exactly.'

He moved nearer, his green eyes fixed on her earnest face. 'Are you always so discerning, Christine? You're so young, yet sometimes there's a wordless wisdom in your eyes. And such composure.' His voice became taunting again. 'I wonder what it would take to shake it?'

'Are you amusing yourself by trying to?' She backed away from him slightly. 'I promised to look after you but I hope you aren't relying on me for entertainment?'

'At least,' he retorted, eyes glinting, 'you must be willing to wish me luck, *bon voyage*, or whatever with a kiss?'

Christine's pale cheeks flamed. 'You aren't away yet and that last privilege surely belongs to your fiancée.'

'She won't be around, as I've told you.'

Christine realised he was merely teasing her, but, if he hadn't been, she knew she couldn't trust herself to kiss him. As far as Richard was concerned, she was too aware of her own limitations. If she even went near him, she was likely to end up sobbing in his arms.

'I'm going to bed.' She shrugged, deciding to ignore him though her heart was thumping.

'Is that an invitation?'

'No!' She glared at Richard, wondering what had got into him. She had never known him quite like this before. He was usually cold and cynical. 'It's going to be impossible if you go on like this.'

'Where's your sense of humour?' he grinned, and, as if using his own as an excuse, he hauled her into his arms before she could move.

'Maybe I'm not acting like a proper employer,' he muttered abstractedly, 'but the circumstances must be unusual.'

'Richard . . .!'

Her protest was lost as his mouth found hers, parting her lips hungrily, his arms closing tightly about her, crushing her to the length of his powerful body. His kisses deepened, drugging her with a pleasure she tried to fight, but when her clenched hands found their way to his shoulders they came up against unyielding muscle.

He was so strong, she thought, achingly, despairingly. She didn't think he meant to hurt her but she was equally certain that he was using her to drown an unconscious longing for another woman. She could sense the emotion running through him, an emotion resembling her own despair, if not from the same root.

He loved Pearl. He couldn't face either being unable to see her, or the coming disruption of his life, and, by some strange twist of fate, she was able to help him to forget all of it, at least for a little while.

Christine knew this, yet it hurt to hear her suspicions put into words.

'You do something to me,' he groaned against her lips. 'You have the effect of strong wine, you help me to forget . . .'

'You have to be sensible,' she whispered, trembling.

'Sensible?' He laughed harshly. 'I've been sensible all my life and look where it's got me!'

She couldn't follow him; she had an idea he was talking of things about which she knew nothing. 'All the same,' she began, when to her surprised relief he suddenly pushed her away from him.

'Okay, Christine,' he grated. 'But no lectures, please. I'm in no mood for them.'

Instinctively she obeyed, her intuition warning her not to provoke him. She didn't even protest when he suggested a drink, other than to offer to make coffee.

'Coffee would only keep you awake.' He sighed. 'And you'd probably spend the night thinking things of me I wouldn't appreciate. I'd rather leave tomorrow knowing you thought well of me.'

Despite herself, Christine grinned. 'You're becoming maudlin,' she teased, accepting the sherry he gave her and taking a sip.

His eyes rested on her lips. 'I even envy that glass.'

She lowered it quickly, colour washing under her skin as her heart skipped a beat. Recognising the strain behind the self-mockery on his face, she realised he was trying as hard as she was to pretend that tomorrow was just another day. If he had been guilty of acting and speaking out of character, it might be no more than any other man might have done in such a situation. Everyone reacted in some way to a traumatic experience in their lives. Richard might be a hard, unflappable business man but he was also human. Very human! Christine gulped and swallowed the remains of her drink in one go, as it suddenly became imperative to escape him.

'Christine——' As if guessing her intentions, his voice was low and pleading as she put her glass down. 'Stay a while longer, don't leave me.'

'I must,' she breathed, never dreaming that he would really try to stop her, but his arms went around her, drawing her close again before she had taken two steps. He removed her ability to actively object by pressing swift kisses over her face and neck, her cheeks and closed eyelids, until her mouth grew so indescribably envious that she turned it up to him blatantly.

She hadn't realised how intoxicating his kisses could be. The taste she'd had of them before had given her only a vague idea. She gasped as his tongue gently parted her unsteady lips and his hands bared her shoulders as he unbuttoned her blouse. Then the same tongue which had invaded her mouth began playing erotic games with the pulse in her throat and tracing the fragile lines of her collar bone.

Christine shivered, desire beating hotly in her body, melting the pit of her stomach, weakening her legs so that she had to lean against him or fall. She heard him groan under his breath, then he was picking her up, carrying her to the sofa, sitting down with her over his knees so he could remove her blouse completely.

She sighed as his mouth touched her breasts, reponding to his fierce need with an innocent hunger of her own. A white hot pleasure surged through her as he caressed her pink nipples until they hardened betrayingly. She shuddered but no longer tried to escape him. No man had ever touched her so intimately, or with such hungry expertise. No man had ever aroused her to such an inexpressible state of yearning. She was overwhelmed by a growing excitement different from anything she had ever known.

Richard's breath thickened. From being idly teasing, his mouth sought and covered hers, burning with a strength of desire that seemed to catch him unawares.

'I want you,' he groaned, his arms tightening roughly. 'I've ached for you for days—weeks!'

His words, muttered against her lips, were unintelligible to Christine's dazed ears and her arms slipping eagerly around his neck must have seemed a silent confirmation that she shared his impatience. Her senses reeled beneath his kisses, the almost desperate passion in his voice, the urgent glide of his palms over her bare flesh. Her lips parted, her head fell back as the fires he aroused inside her threatened to make her forget everything else.

Being at the mercy of such searing emotions, perhaps it wasn't surprising that fear should suddenly seize her—the instinctive, self-protective apprehension of inexperience. Like a cold shower of rain, something reminded her that the man whose arms she was in was engaged to another woman and could only be amusing himself. He must have decided, because of Ken, that she was promiscuous, and as keen to indulge herself in what men referred to as a little on the side, as he was. His body was pressing against hers in a way that brought colour to her cheeks, his intentions so suddenly clear that her heart began pounding, less with passion than with genuine fright.

She began to struggle, her eyes burning with tears as hot as his ruthless lips, and when he felt their wetness on his face, he drew back. He groaned in unconscious protest, then stiffened as sanity returned to him in a rush. She saw him shake his head savagely, as if to clear it.

As abruptly as he had taken hold of her, he let her go, easing himself away from her to his feet. 'You'd better get to bed,' he said tonelessly, his eyes bleak.

'Richard!' Puzzled by his expression, she scrambled up beside him, laying an uncertain hand on his arm.

Impatiently he shook it off. 'Just go,' he snapped, so harshly that she didn't wait to be told again.

It was just as well, she thought, on her way to her room. What a fool she might have made of herself if he had given her a chance to put into words feelings so new to her that she could never have logically expressed them. If she had stammered out that it was her growing love for him that had made her respond to him as she had, she could just imagine his embarrassment. That night, Christine's prayers were as confused as her thoughts. She prayed that Richard would decide to stay in London, then she prayed he would come back to her.

The next morning he departed early, after issuing endless instructions to Christine regarding her personal safety, leaving himself little time to reach the airport. The taxi waited patiently and as she watched it finally disappear along the drive, she realised how isolated a place like Cragend must seem to someone used to living in cities. This was why Richard was always so anxious about her being here on her own. Her attempts to assure him she would be quite safe had fallen on deaf ears. If she had been ready and willing, she was sure he would have hustled her into the taxi with him.

Last night might never have happened. At breakfast he had been crisp and very distant, even when lecturing her on locking doors and windows and keeping a look out for strangers. She had resolved to tell him she wouldn't be here when he came back again but the thought of him returning to an empty house, ill and needing her, defeated her. In the harsh light of another day, she found that, with a little sensible determination, a few kisses could be reduced to something of no importance. When she looked at Richard's cold, unfriendly face, the feeling they had induced had about as much substance as a mirage.

It was three weeks before he returned, not the three days he had predicted. Christine passed the time fretting about why he was taking so long and wondering if she would ever see him again. Harry rang, telling her to be patient and that Richard was all right, but he refused to discuss him. But for Ken calling twice, with his new girlfriend, she might have gone out of her mind.

Christine wasn't hurt that Ken had found another girl, for, though he had often hinted that he would have liked them to be closer, there had never been anything but friendship between them. When he brought Pam, a lively little redhead to see her, she was puzzled by her own reactions until she realised it wasn't pique she felt, but relief. She refused to believe that it had anything to do with Richard.

The first she knew of Richard being on his way home, was when Harry rang from Aberdeen.

'Get the kettle on, honey,' he laughed, doing an amusing impersonation of his English hosts. 'No one makes a cuppa like you, love.'

'Oh, Harry,' she giggled to a dead line, tears streaming unheeded down her cheeks. 'How long will you be?'

No one answered, of course, and, as she belatedly realised that he had rung off, she was galvanised into action. Richard was coming home; she was suddenly full of dread and excitement. She forgot all the reasons why she shouldn't care so much for him, she could only think that in an hour or two she was going to see him again.

When he and Harry arrived, she ran out to meet them, unable to hide her relief. Yet, as she halted abruptly by the taxi and watched Richard climb out unaided, she couldn't speak, her heart felt like bursting. He was exactly the same, apart from a narrow bandage over his eyes, but his senses were more alert than ever.

'Christine?' He turned his head so accurately to the exact spot where she was standing, she could scarcely believe it.

'Richard.' She faltered, as Harry settled with the taxi driver. 'It's good to have you home again. It seems a long time . . .'

'I was delayed.'

'Oh, I see . . .'

'More than I can,' he snapped, though with no self-pity in his voice. 'Could we get inside?'

'Yes, of course. I'm sorry,' she apologised, automatically putting a hand out to guide him as he started towards the gardens. He seemed about to shake it off, then sighed grimly and allowed her to turn him in the right direction.

'All I need is a little practice,' he said. 'I'll be able to manage indoors.'

She wasn't really surprised when he did. She would not put anything past him, he was that kind of man. She watched with a rather dazed expression in her eyes as he negotiated the hall and lounge without mishap. He even found his way to his new bedroom to see whether the new bed had arrived. The only thing he stumbled into there was the chair Christine had moved from upstairs while he had been away and had forgotten to tell him about.

'It's a nice bed,' she said tentatively, after he had cursed a little over the chair.

'I'll give you my opinion in the morning,' he said curtly. 'I hope you and your boyfriend haven't been trying it out.'

'You never know,' she retorted, trying to pretend she was amused.

Her obvious attempt to humour him appeared only to infuriate. 'You don't have to follow me around, Christine. I'd rather fall over things until I get my bearings. I'm not completely helpless and I think I'm tough enough to survive a few knocks.'

Christine knew when she was defeated, at least temporarily. With a last tearful glance at the proud angle of his head, she turned and fled.

Harry, coming in through the front door with the last of the luggage, dumped it in the hall and followed her into the kitchen.

'I'm making tea,' she said thickly, keeping her back to him so that he couldn't see her face.

He sat on the edge of the table, swinging his leg and watching her while she plugged in the kettle. 'He will be all right,' he said softly. 'Don't worry.'

'It's difficult not to,' she whispered, an unconscious break in her voice. 'Somehow I can't bear to see him so helpless.'

Harry laughed with gentle irony. 'It's not grammatically correct but you'll be amazed at how helpless he isn't. There's a lot of truth in the old adage that some can see more with their eyes closed than others with them wide open.'

'But he has no choice!' she whispered.

'I know. I'm just warning you. And whatever you do, don't let him sense you're sorry for him. He hates pity.'

Christine swallowed. 'Is sympathy the same thing?'

'Often it seems like the same thing.' Harry shrugged. 'Depends how one wishes to interpret it. Richard's going to be prickly for a while.'

'Harry?' She swung around quickly. 'He won't want me asking questions, but when he went away he said it would be for a few days and it's been three weeks. You say that he's going to be all right but I can't help feeling that there have been complications.'

'He had a small operation,' he revealed. 'But nothing serious. We think we've definitely corrected the trouble. However,' he said carefully, 'this is just between you and me. I'd rather you didn't mention what I've told you to Ric or anyone.'

'How—long will be it before you can be quite certain about him?' she asked.

'Not long.' He smiled.

She prayed that for Richard's sake, it wouldn't be.

Harry stayed two days and she missed him when he went. He stood between her and Richard's black moods and she wasn't sure how she would cope once he was gone.

The first morning after Harry left, Richard asked whether she would do some typing for him. Having been warned by Harry not to let him do too much, she didn't know what to say. If she agreed, she could be doing him more harm than good, yet how could she refuse when he knew she could type and he was the boss?

'Once I get used to doing everything in the dark I won't need you,' he said tersely, mistaking her doubtful silence for a reluctance to take on anything extra.

'You're only allowed to work a short time each day,' she retorted. 'You're probably doing more than enough already.'

'That is why I'm asking you to help me out.' He smiled glibly. 'I won't do more than I'm able to, I promise.'

What sort of a promise was that? Christine sighed as she left what she was doing and followed him to the study. She knew she could be of some use to him, if only she could be as sure she was doing the right thing. Harry had said that she must learn to put her foot down. Unfortunately, she had forgotten to ask him how.

While Harry had been there, Richard had merely kept in touch with his London office by telephone, and she had thought that he would continue to limit himself to this and to dictating a few letters for her to type. She was soon to discover how far from the mark she was. No sooner had Harry's dust settled on the drive than tapes began arriving from London and the telephone which had once observed short silences began ringing practically non-stop.

On top of typing numerous letters and reports, not to mention technical data with its signs and symbols about which she knew nothing, Christine was called on to cope whenever the tape recorder stuck and Richard wasn't able to adjust the delicate mechanism without seeing it. There was also a lot of information to file.

At first, Richard lost his temper when she couldn't keep up, then he calmed down and began to take a perverse interest in teaching her all the things he considered she should know. She had a good brain and a quick intelligence which seemed to please him; within a week they were working together in surprising harmony. Christine didn't pretend that she was coming anywhere near being indispensable to him but she was satisfied that she could keep up with his basic requirements. She also felt that her ability to absorb what he taught her had restored a wavering faith in his own abilities and, at the same time, helped him to combat the constant sense of frustration which his enforced blindness caused.

That she was able to help him, she had to admit delighted her perhaps more than the actual job. Yet she enjoyed the challenge of it, as well as the sense of sharing. Often on a cold, dark afternoon, when they were closeted together in the study, in constant touch with the outside world yet completely isolated from it, the feeling of close companionship they shared warmed her incredibly. It was strangely soothing to a heart frequently chilled by the certain knowledge that he loved someone else.

One afternoon, he threw down his pen and came over to where she was busy typing. Raising her head, she watched him approach, the sureness of his movements never failing to amaze her.

'How about going for a walk?' he suggested. 'I don't know about you but I could do with some fresh air.'

She smiled eagerly though she knew he couldn't see. 'I'd love to. Oh, but,' her voice fell with disappointment, 'aren't you expecting that important call from London?'

'Just from my secretary.' He shrugged. 'She'll ring back if she can't get me straight away. Anyway,' his broad shoulders lifted again, 'I don't really care that much if I miss it.'

Noticing the lines of weariness on his face, Christine felt worried. 'Wouldn't it be better if you had a proper secretary here?' she asked anxiously. 'You know I wouldn't mind looking after her and you'd be able to rest more.'

'Maybe do more,' he grunted. 'I stick to Harry's rules, don't I? I only work an hour or two each day.'

'Yesterday it was six.'

'Oh, so we're counting now, are we?' he muttered sarcastically. 'Well, even if I collapse, Ida isn't coming to Cragend. Besides, she's indispensable in London, someone has to run that end while I'm here. Now come on.' He ran an impatient hand over his hair, 'Let's get outside while there's still light. Not,' he added derisively, 'that it would make any difference to me but I don't want you taking the wrong path so that we finish up in the loch.'

Christine sometimes despised herself for loving their walks through the forest, when Richard had to hold her arm and rely on her completely. In another sense, it hurt her to see him so dependent on her, especially when she knew he hated it. It grieved her, too, when things happened to defeat him about which she could do nothing, such as Pearl forgetting to ring. He didn't say anything but once she had caught him resting his head against the back of a chair in the lounge, an expression of such bleakness on his face that she had known immediately what was wrong. If she could have got hold of Pearl that day she might have shaken her!

As they walked by the loch on that December afternoon, somehow they began talking about Christmas. Usually Christine described the various species of wild life she saw as they went along. When Richard had first returned, with his blindfold on, he had informed her almost savagely that if she thought she was going to become his eyes, she was mistaken.

'I refuse to be led around like that dog of yours,' he had snapped. 'I suppose you've been looking up all your bird and tree books, while I've been away, and thinking up interesting ways of describing the weather. Well, you can forget about it. I can do without all that for a few months.'

She hadn't mentioned that she didn't need to consult books to be able to describe what was going on about her but obediently she had talked of other things. It was Richard who began asking about the different sounds he heard while they were out, which way the wind was blowing and whether it looked like rain. From what seemed an unconscious resentment of his surroundings, he began to give the impression that he was, perhaps just as unconsciously, growing fond of them, and, despite his handicap, she felt instinctively, as the days of his stay lengthened, that he was finding a kind of peace here which he had never known before.

'Is Mrs Kristol still coming for Christmas?' Christine asked, as Richard wondered idly if they would have a white one. She tried to sound cheerful. He had grown terribly sensitive about her voice. He could often tell from it, far too astutely, exactly how she was feeling and she didn't want him to suspect how much she dreaded Pearl's visit. If Pearl had loved him it would have been another matter. Perhaps she did love him, in a way, but Christine suspected she was entirely self-centred. She hated to think how easily and carelessly Richard's fiancée might destroy his hard-won equanimity.

'She'll be here.' Christine heard him reply grimly.

Knowing he couldn't be looking forward to Pearl seeing him as he was, she squeezed his hand involuntarily. 'I bet she can hardly wait.'

'To get away again, most likely.'

'I'm sure that's not true.' Christine hoped it wasn't. 'We must try and do something special for her.'

'Last year,' he said drily, 'she was in New York. We can't compete with that.'

'We may get snow.' Christine refused to let him be depressed. 'The mountains are really beautiful then, and the fir trees, especially those around the loch, look magnificent.'

Richard's mouth merely twisted, but whether he was unimpressed by what she said or thinking of Pearl, she couldn't tell.

'I'll put up some decorations,' she offered eagerly. 'The ones we always use are still in the attic. I checked the other day.'

'For God's sake, Christine!' he exclaimed. 'You had no business going up there alone. You could have broken your neck. Anyway, I wouldn't be able to see them and Pearl probably wouldn't even look at them. She never puts anything up herself—thinks it only makes a mess.'

'Don't you like them?' she asked hollowly.

'That's not the point, is it?' he retorted. 'And don't say I'll know they are there, because I couldn't care less.'

Guiding him carefully over a piece of boggy ground, an abstracted frown creased Christine's smooth brow. 'How about when you get married and have children? You'll have to put something up then.'

He laughed cynically. 'I give you top marks for persevering, Christine. As Pearl doesn't like children, I don't suppose we'll have any.'

'Don't you like them either?' Christine asked, unaware of how shocked she sounded.

'What man doesn't want a son and heir?' He shrugged. 'But as it's the woman who usually looks after it, I think it should be left to her to decide. Some women might prefer motherhood to modelling but not Pearl.'

A lot of couples were quite happy without children. For various reasons, often financial ones, they didn't have any. Christine realised that but Richard's marriage sounded as if it might also be barren in other ways . . .

Unconsciously she shivered, and Richard, feeling the tremor in her slight body, disentangled his arm from hers and draped it around her shoulders.

'What is it?' he asked anxiously. 'Are you cold?'

'No . . . I mean, yes.' She almost missed the excuse. 'It's getting dark, too. Perhaps we'd better get back. I'll make tea . . .'

'Do you know,' he mused, as they were sitting in front of a roaring fire eating crumpets oozing with butter and Christine's rich fruit cake, 'I could get addicted to this kind of life. Even without my eyes, this is my idea of heaven.'

Christine glanced at him somewhat incredulously and when, just for once, she was glad he couldn't see her expression, he startled her by enquiring, 'Why so surprised?'

It might be foolish to pretend she wasn't. 'I should have thought nightclubs and jet-set travel, witty conversation and glamorous women were more in your line,' she replied flippantly.

'They never have been,' he replied coldly. 'Though there's nothing wrong with any of it in moderation. What gave you that idea?'

'I don't really know,' she confessed, cutting him a second slab of fruit cake. 'I suppose the kind of business you're in, travelling all over the world, living in luxury . . .'

He laughed drily. 'One's way of life is often ruled by circumstances, I agree, and it's often easier to conform than to kick over the traces. As long as nothing has interfered with my work, I haven't really paid much attention to my private life.'

'Y-you've managed to acquire a fiancée.'

'I've never lived like this before,' he said, as if the room and the fire, the two of them together interested him far more than Pearl. 'Come here, Christine,' he commanded huskily, putting down his cup and holding out his hand.

Suddenly the telephone rang. 'I'll get it,' Christine cried, pretending she hadn't heard him. The way he had made his request laced it with the kind of intimacy she knew she would be wiser to ignore.

'If it's Ida, tell her I'll speak to her tomorrow,' he called after her.

It wasn't Ida, it was Pearl.

'How is he?' she asked quickly, interrupting Christine after asking for Richard, while Christine was saying that she would fetch him.

'Very well,' Christine replied shortly. 'Apart from his

eyes.' She forced herself to add, 'He's looking forward to your visit.'

Pearl's impatient sigh was clearly audible. 'I suppose I'll have to turn up for Christmas, though I'd much rather spend it in London. Do you think he's going to be permanently blind?'

The callous bluntness of Pearl's question made Christine wince. 'I'm not his medical adviser,' she said tersely.

'I thought you might have heard something,' Pearl grumbled.

'If you wait a moment, you can ask him yourself,' Christine retorted, laying down the receiver carefully and wishing that it had been anyone but Pearl who had rung. Judging by the mood she was in, Richard was almost certain to be hurt.

CHAPTER FIVE

WHEN Richard returned from speaking to Pearl he didn't appear to be upset. Christine realised why as soon as he sat down.

'She's coming for Christmas.' He smiled. 'I told her that we were talking about it this afternoon, but I'd forgotten that it's only two weeks away.'

Christine couldn't see his eyes but she could guess from his smile how pleased he was. 'Yes,' she replied woodenly.

He frowned, drawing his own conclusions from the heaviness of her voice and saying coaxingly. 'If we aren't putting up decorations, at least we can go to town on something to eat. Any suggestions?'

Christine drew an unsteady breath, glad that the thread of intimacy between them was broken again and grateful that he was keeping his distance. He was trying to be nice, maybe indirectly for Pearl's sake, but surely it was up to her to meet him halfway?

'I made a cake and a plum pudding while you were in London but I didn't order any poultry,' she said.

'Is it possible to get anything locally?'

'The Macleods, of Inveru, that's a farm a few miles away, will let us have something. We've left it a bit late but they're very obliging.'

'And we could go on to Inverness and see what we can find there. You'll have to do the seeing, I'm afraid, but I should still be good for carrying.'

Richard's dry remarks might bring tears to her eyes but at least he was smiling. If Pearl continued to make him smile, Christine thought that she could forgive her anything. The following day, after talking to his secretary in London, he insisted they set off to do the shopping immediately.

She had to drive the car but he managed very well otherwise. He was proud and he had a lot of what her father would have called guts. Seeing him reflected in the mirrors of shops, so tall and handsome, holding her arm lightly, she began to realise just how much courage he had. And he might need even more, she thought achingly. Wasn't there a possibility that he could be permanently blind? Harry merely mentioned complicated eye strain but Pearl had sounded very suspicious, and surely she would be in a good position to know?

Christine considered that they shopped far too extravagantly. If it had been left to her, their purchases would have been modest, out of habit. Richard insisted on visiting the best supermarkets and stores and he had an expert knowledge of food and wine. She soon gave up pretending that some things weren't in stock or that she couldn't find them, for he immediately asked for them and had often otherwise invisible managers and staff falling over themselves to get what he wanted.

At last she said, 'If you buy anything more, we shan't be able to get in the car ourselves. As it is, I don't think I'll have any rear vision.'

'All right.' He laughed, as if he could actually see the indignation in her eyes. 'Let's call it a day and find something to eat. I haven't felt so hungry in weeks.'

'Where would you like to go?' she asked without thinking.

He shrugged. 'At the moment, one place is very much like another to me, but,' he teased, 'find somewhere cosy, then we can sit and tick off our purchases like an old married couple.'

Christine's cheeks were still pink when they were ordering their meal in the only restaurant with which she was familiar in the city. She had been here before with Ken. She was pleased that the extra fresh air and the change from Cragend had given Richard an appetite; he hadn't been eating well lately, though he still wasn't thin. Her eyes lingered over his strongly proportioned body. It was his face, with its frequent lines of strain, which worried her most. Perhaps when Pearl came he would relax more as well as being happier.

She went on looking at him with unconscious absorption throughout the meal, liking the way his jeans hugged his lean hips, the way the jacket he wore over his shirt sat on his broad shoulders. She also admired how he coped with the various courses. He stuck to things that didn't require cutting up and managed perfectly. Sometimes she felt so proud of him that she wanted to throw her arms around him and hug him. Which would never do, she cautioned herself severely. If she did that, he would immediately believe she saw him as someone to be pitied. Occasionally she did pity him, she admitted, but not in the way to which she knew he would object.

She was startled when Ken paused by their table, just as they had finished eating.

'Hello, Chris.' He grinned, his eyes flickering curiously to Richard. 'It's been a long time.'

'Yes, it has been,' she replied, smiling at him warmly. She was pleased to see him but rather nervous over Richard's reactions. Sometimes she had a feeling that he didn't like Ken.

He must have recognised Ken's voice, for he stiffened and startled her by saying curtly. 'The name's Christine, Granger.'

'I've always called her Chris,' Ken said blithely. 'How are you, sir?'

'Not in my dotage,' Richard snapped between his teeth. 'There's no need for the sirs, either. Christine and I are just going.'

'We've been doing some Christmas shopping,' Christine put in hastily, feeling sorry for Ken and annoyed that Richard should be behaving with such uncharacteristic churlishness. 'Mr Kingsley's fiancée is going to be staying at Cragend for Christmas.'

'Ah.' Having a much thicker skin than Christine, Ken

smiled cheerfully. 'You may get some time off then? When Mr Kingsley has someone else to look after him.'

'Ken,' she warned with a quick glance at Richard's angry face.

'Well, won't you?'

Was Ken really as stupid as he appeared to be? 'Give me a ring,' she said quickly, hurrying after Richard as he strode towards the cash desk with a complete disregard for his personal safety.

In the car, he said grimly. 'Does your friend Ken think I'm deaf as well as blind?'

'We both know that you are neither,' she snapped, for once not prepared to humour him. 'So you can stop being so bloody minded and feeling sorry for yourself.'

There was an electric silence, then just when she expected to be annihilated, he laughed. True it was a rather grudging laugh but she preferred it to his anger.

'I suppose you have a point there,' he conceded. 'However, I'm not sure how Pearl will feel about baby-sitting. I'd rather you didn't make any definite arrangements.'

'I'd be surprised if Ken has anything definite in mind,' she replied, evenly. She wondered if she should mention Ken's girlfriend, then decided against it, as Ken seemed about the only defence she had left. Christine might not have been able to explain, even to herself, what she meant by that but she thought it more prudent to let Richard believe her affections were engaged elsewhere.

When Pearl arrived at Cragend it was snowing, great white flakes driven by a rising wind. The taxi driver refused a cup of coffee, saying he'd be lucky to get back to Aberdeen. Christine, who had helped Richard outside, saw the size of the note he crushed into the man's hand. Pearl pretended not to notice.

'I hope I'll be able to get back to London,' Christine heard Pearl grumbling, as she let go of Richard's arm to give him a chance to greet his fiancée.

'It probably won't last,' Richard grunted, as they turned to go indoors.

Christine watched with her mouth half open. Richard had made no move to kiss Pearl, neither had she kissed him. Her temper flared. Didn't Pearl realise that Richard couldn't see her?

'You haven't kissed him!' she hissed before she could stop herself.

Having meant her remark for Pearl's ears alone, she was mortified when Richard immediately grabbed hold of Pearl and kissed her soundly.

'No need to overdo it!' Pearl snapped furiously, disentangling herself fastidiously, with a venomous glance at Christine. 'We don't have to provide a floor show for your housekeeper. I was quite aware that I hadn't kissed my fiancé, Miss Colwell. I was merely waiting for a little more privacy.'

Christine buried her burning face in Pearl's luggage, wishing it would open up and swallow her. 'I—I'm sorry,' she gulped.

'Let's get inside,' Richard said shortly, sounding as if he had been playing a game and grown tired of it. 'I'm sure Pearl will want a rest before dinner.'

'I'm exhausted,' Pearl agreed, the discontent in her voice audible to Christine as she staggered behind with Pearl's cases. 'Really, Richard, even though you can't see, I don't understand why you couldn't have come to London. I've had to turn down several promising invitations.'

How would she expect Richard to enjoy them? Christine ground her small white teeth as she hauled the largest case upstairs. What on earth did Pearl have in it? More important, how long did she intend staying?

'I hope I'm next to Mr Kingsley?' Pearl caught up with her impatiently.

'You're in the same room as you were last time,' Christine replied politely. Let Pearl discover for herself where Richard slept now—or let her ask him! With a mutinous glance of which she wasn't particularly proud, she left Pearl quickly, after informing her coolly that dinner was at seven.

Pearl came down at ten past and didn't apologise. Christine kept the soup warm and Richard calm by telling him that there was nothing which would spoil. That wasn't strictly true but nothing came to much harm in ten minutes.

'I don't want a repeat of all that nonsense about eating in the kitchen,' Richard said curtly. 'You'll eat in the dining-room with us, whether you like it or not.'

'I thought you and Mrs Kristol would have so much to talk about that you'd rather be alone.'

He didn't answer, other than to tighten his lips in a 'do it or else' fashion, as Pearl swept into the room.

Occasionally, when Christine remembered how plain she was, she was almost glad that Richard couldn't see. This evening, when she saw how beautiful Pearl looked, she felt a fierce surge of relief, of which she was quickly ashamed. As far as Richard was concerned, all Pearl's efforts must be wasted.

She wore a beautiful lamé dress of silver and gold, so tight that she appeared to have been poured into it. Her hair was piled on top of her head, which, with her high heels, made her nearly as tall as Richard. She was dazzling and very much aware of it.

'Such a shame that you can't see me, darling,' she purred, kissing him lightly on the cheek.

'My nose still functions,' he murmured wryly. 'What's that scent you're wearing? Ummm.' Catching hold of her arm, he bent his head to her bare shoulder. 'You smell delicious.'

'You should know, you bought it for me in New York last summer.' Pearl laughed, 'Don't you remember?'

'So good of you to remind me so beautifully of happier days,' he said softly, deftly pulling out a chair for her.

Christine simmered gently with the soup as she gave it a final stir before serving. Pig! She hid her heartache with anger. He had a nerve to insinuate, as he sometimes did, that he was practically a social non-starter, when such glibness of tongue wasn't acquired without years of practice.

Throughout dinner she listened as Pearl entertained Richard with languid accounts of her latest assignments and the parties to which she had been. She seemed to know everyone whom she considered mattered and many of her comments were very amusing. She had a malicious but very sharp wit and if Richard didn't respond very heartily, at least he didn't retreat into himself, Christine noticed, as he was wont to do in the evenings when she tried to talk to him.

When Pearl eventually ran out of stories, she said disparagingly, 'I don't know how you survive living here, Richard. By the time you return to London it will take you weeks before you're fit for normal society again.'

Christine blazed quickly. 'The people in these parts are very normal, Pearl. Richard could only benefit from living among them.'

'No need to get uptight about it, Christine.' Richard made it plain that he wouldn't put up with her being rude to his fiancée.

'Sorry,' Christine mumbled, feeling slightly sick as she realised that he was right. The trouble was, Pearl was wrong for him. She would never make him a good wife, not the kind he might be going to need, anyway.

She watched, trying to control her bitterness, when, as if to make amends for her rudeness, Richard groped for Pearl's hand. Pearl made no attempt to meet him halfway but let him fumble until he found her. Even then, she withdrew her hand quickly after allowing him to give hers a comforting squeeze.

Christine drew a sharp breath. Wasn't Pearl at all sensitive to his feelings? She must know how she was affecting him. Richard must be very much in love with her, for it wasn't like him to knock over the salt and drop his fork or to spill a drop of wine on his shirt, which, to Christine's disgust, made Pearl's eyes grow cold with distaste.

At ten they were still talking and Christine went to bed after spending an hour in the kitchen stuffing the turkey for the next day. She didn't mind being tired, she wanted to be, as weariness helped her to forget last Christmas, when her father had been alive. It also helped her to forget that the only man who had ever stirred her deeply was in the lounge, probably making love to another woman.

After reading for a long time and tossing and turning even longer, she still couldn't sleep and decided to go downstairs again and heat some milk. She had just reached the kitchen but hadn't put on the light when she heard Pearl and Richard coming out of the lounge and saying good night. Pearl didn't see her and she was sure that Richard wasn't aware of her presence, as they exchanged a few abrupt words before Richard went to his room—alone. Christine wasn't foolish enough to conclude from the scene she had witnessed that they had quarrelled, but there was nothing in the stiffness of Richard's back, or the flounce to Pearl's as she stalked upstairs, to suggest that they had recently made love.

Christine was up early on Christmas Day, having slept better than she had expected to. The sun was shining and the ground outside was white. For a moment she gazed at it with enchanted delight. It had been snowing last night, but she hadn't dared to hope for a white Christmas.

'Richard!' Dragging on her dressing-gown, she ran down to his room, too excited to stop and think. 'It's such a beautiful morning—everything's white—Oh . . .!'

Instead of being in bed, he was sitting on the edge of it, wearing only a pair of briefs. Heat flooded through her as she fell back with a gasp. 'Oh, I'm sorry, I didn't think you would be g-getting dressed . . .'

'Don't panic, Christine.' To her relief, yet further embarrassment, he laughed. 'I'm really quite decent, you don't have to blush.'

'I'm not,' she protested then realised that her cheeks were hot. 'Well . . . Oh, I'll leave you to get on with it . . .'

'Christine!' He halted her mockingly as she turned. 'Haven't you forgotten to wish me a Happy Christmas? It's customary.'

She supposed it was. Clearing her throat, she whispered, 'Happy Christmas, Richard.'

'Not from so far away,' he said softly. 'It would be much more satisfactory if I could hear what you are saying. Surely at a time like this, with me like this, you could give me a kiss?'

As usual, he was trading outrageously on her sympathy. Christine stared at him disapprovingly but she couldn't resist the arms which were held out, somewhat pathetically, in the wrong direction.

'Oh, Richard!' she choked and in a moment she was in his arms, wrapping her own around him convulsively. 'I've nothing much for you but I would like to wish you a perfect recovery, perfect health.'

'A kiss might be worth more than anything else,' he muttered thickly, claiming it, without further ado, from trembling lips.

Christine thought that she wouldn't have minded dying right then, as she must be very near heaven. Crazy, rapturous thoughts whirled through her mind, then they were blotted out in a surge of ecstasy. Thrusting her bare arms around his neck, she held him so tightly that they might have been as one. The pressure of Richard's mouth deepened and he strained her closer. It was a few moments of absolute wildness, as recklessly urgent arms and bodies threatened to get out of hand.

Then suddenly, as a door banged loudly upstairs, she was thrust abruptly from him. Christine didn't speak—she couldn't. She merely turned blindly and left him to stumble back to her room.

Pearl was again late in coming down and when she

did, she viewed the brightness of the morning with a jaundiced eye.

'I didn't buy you a present,' she told Richard, kissing him coolly. 'I knew you wouldn't want me wasting my hard-earned cash on something you couldn't see.'

Christine had given him a sweater which she had secretly knitted in her room, in a soft, comfortable wool. As he was short of them, she had thought it a sensible idea. If he couldn't see it, it was something he could feel and wear. She ignored the pleasure and love that had gone into the making of it. Why hadn't Pearl given him something like that? She looked at the other girl bleakly. The shops of London must be full of similar things, if she had used her imagination.

'Christine wants to go to church,' Richard said, after giving Pearl a beautiful diamond bracelet with which she didn't look terribly impressed. 'Lunch won't be until two o'clock, unless you care to cook it?'

'Church?' Pearl echoed blankly.

'We could go, too, if you like?' Richard suggested cheerfully.

'I'd rather go somewhere for a drink.' She frowned.

'You might need more than a drink if you attempted to drive all the way to the nearest hotel with the roads as they are this morning, Mrs Kristol,' Christine said quickly, mindful of Richard's safety.

'Oh, well.' Pearl smiled suddenly. 'I suppose I could wear my new mink. It won't be completely wasted, the minister may appreciate it.'

Christine saw Richard's brows rise slightly and wondered if he was wondering, as she was, how Pearl could hint in one breath of being short of money and in the next, of possessing a coat which usually cost thousands.

Later, Christine wished she had been allowed to go to church alone. If Richard hadn't insisted on coming, Pearl would have stayed with him. Pearl grumbled all the way that the roads were atrocious, that she was cold, that Richard was thoughtless and that Scotland at this time of year—at any time of the year—was hopeless! During the service, Christine had to concentrate on keeping murderous thoughts at bay, which she was sure weren't at all Christian.

Lunch surprised Christine by being a great success, for she had heard that if the cook was in a bad mood, the food was invariably ruined. Pearl's incessant grousing, which had continued even returning from church, had depressed her so much, that she found it difficult to concentrate on what she was doing.

Richard appeared to appreciate everything; even Pearl congratulated Christine grudgingly, though she obviously enjoyed the wine most. What sorrows was she drowning? Christine glanced at her frequently throughout the meal, for which Richard, as usual, had insisted she joined them. The wine, while cheering Pearl up, couldn't hide her prevailing dissatisfaction. She complained constantly that there was nothing to do and that the church had been so cold that she was sure she would never be warm again.

Taking the coffee cups back to the kitchen, she left the other two in the lounge, in front of the roaring fire Pearl demanded to counteract the effects of the chill she believed she had caught. The rest of the day stretched in front of Christine and seemed as long as a year, which she couldn't understand, as usually her days weren't long enough.

After washing the dishes and putting them away, she decided to go for a walk. Aware, from a certain dampness in the air, that the snow might be gone by the morning, she had an urge to make the most of it. After finding her wellingtons and coat, she was just letting herself out of the back door when she heard Richard's step in the kitchen.

'Christine?' He paused in that uncertain way that went straight to her heart.

'I was just going out,' she said, letting him know where she was by closing the door again. 'Did you want something?'

His mouth tightened for a moment, then he shook his head. 'I thought you might be going for a walk and I hoped to go with you. See,' he raised a hand to his chest, 'I'm wearing the pullover you gave me. It's lovely and warm.'

His slightly taut smile tugged even more at her heartstrings, so that she had to harden herself against him. 'It looks very nice,' she said coolly. 'Is Mrs Kristol getting ready as well?'

'No, she's staying in,' he replied curtly. 'She's not what you'd call a country girl, Christine, you have to make allowances.'

'Of course,' she replied shortly.

'It's no crime to dislike snow,' she added, making an effort on Pearl's behalf for his sake, as they went outside and he tucked his arm under hers so that she could guide him. 'It's cold and the ground's very icy for walking.'

'You can say that again,' he muttered under his breath as he almost slipped. 'I'll have to hang on harder, I'm afraid. It's a good job my work force can't see me so dependent on a slip of a girl. I'd never live it down. I'd have to sell up.'

'Would it matter?' she teased lightly, while worrying what he would do if he couldn't go back again.

'Sometimes I wonder if it would,' he murmured, almost to himself. 'I'm beginning to like being at Cragend, though peace and quiet have never appealed to me until now.'

'Think how bored you would become with the monotony of living here,' she remarked, again trying to speak lightly. 'You enjoy the challenge of the business-world, organising companies and watching them grow . . .'

'Maybe you're right,' he muttered. 'When changes are forced on one by circumstances, how can one be sure that they're what one really wants?'

'You can't be sure of anything just now, can you?'

'Which isn't always easy to accept,' he said bitterly.

Was he thinking of Pearl? Christine watched a hawk soaring high above the glen, no doubt looking for its tea, but when she described it to Richard he merely nodded, without his usual interest.

'If we hope that he isn't disappointed, some small creature dies, but if he doesn't catch anything, he might.'

'That's life,' Richard muttered soberly.

They walked in silence for a while, Christine thinking that it should be Pearl by his side, not his housekeeper, while Richard's thoughts might have been as forbidding as the loch, so dark did his face grow.

Christine bit her lip as she glanced at him. She didn't want him becoming withdrawn and depressed again. He wouldn't talk to her about what was bothering him but she could guess. Things weren't working out between him and Pearl the way he had hoped they would. The strain of his blindness was coming between them and he blamed himself.

'I think we should be going home.' She had been so engrossed in looking for a solution to his problems that she hadn't noticed the December light failing. 'You don't want Pearl worrying.'

Richard merely shrugged but he turned obediently enough. Unfortunately he turned too quickly and his feet shot out from under him. He landed on his back, pulling Christine down on top of him.

'God!' he groaned aloud, the words jerked out of him. 'If I could only see!'

'Richard!' she gasped, feeling as helpless as he sounded. She shuddered, her hands clenching white. His pain was obvious, if it wasn't exactly physical, and she wondered how much more she could take. She had already witnessed a lot of his suffering, knew of his longing and despair. He was asking more than he knew in believing that she could go on keeping her distance, while she wanted so desperately to comfort him with more than sympathetic silences and a few rallying words.

Yet how could she offer him what she sometimes

sensed he so deeply needed but which she had never offered or given to any man before? Besides, it was something which, by his very commitment to Pearl, he would only want from her.

Shaking visibly, her entire body trembling from the force of the tremors running through her, Christine tried to push away from him but his arm was clamped around her so tightly that she couldn't move.

'Richard?' She wondered what she could say to him. They were lying on the icy snow, the steel of his fingers biting into her, the heat from his body scorching her until she felt she was on fire.

'Richard!' she appealed, but further words were broken off as a traitorous weakness flooded her, sapping her ability to think, while increasing the beat of her heart. She saw the sensual mouth drawing closer as he twisted until he was lying half on top of her, then it ground against hers, as if he was seeking complete oblivion in her lips.

His primitive kiss, with something of the wildness of the elements in it, sparked an answering flame in Christine which consumed all resistance to his touch. In an instant she was clinging to him, her fingers curling around his neck and into the crisp blackness of his hair. He wasn't being kind and gentle but she didn't want him to be like that. She wanted her mouth bruised by his violent kisses. When his hands slid under her coat and sweater and found her breasts, she didn't mind the hurt that they inflicted either. She could only cling to him, shaking, revelling in the searing fire of his embrace, as their kisses became a torturous madness that melted away the pain of his hold.

The force of her emotions must have wrenched tears from her eyes, and feeling them, Richard slowly stiffened. Lifting his mouth from hers, he put a hand to her wet cheek.

'Don't cry, my love,' he muttered huskily. 'I'm sorry. I trade on your soft heart and I can't even pretend I don't know what I'm doing. I don't want you feeling as sorry for me as this though.' Very gently he kissed away her tears.

'Oh, Richard,' she whispered, turning her head until he found her lips. Discounting the ecstasy he aroused, Christine felt that she was giving him, through her kisses, all the sympathy and warmth she knew he would reject if she tried to express it in words.

As if sensing this, he lifted her to her feet with a sigh and began walking again. 'I could do with a drink,' he said, but Christine, feeling cold and rebuffed, knew that it would take more than a drink to solve her problems.

That evening Pearl was dressed in a filmy skirt and a top which was so transparent that it almost took Christine's breath away. She was in the lounge, replenishing the fire when Pearl walked in, and Richard, hearing her faint gasp, asked if something was wrong.

'No,' she told him, 'Mrs Kristol looks so beautiful she startled me, that's all.'

Pearl, for once, bestowed an approving glance on Christine. 'It's a shame you didn't invite a few friends and neighbours this evening, Richard. I bought this outfit specially for you, forgetting that you wouldn't be able to see it.'

Why did Pearl never seem to stop and think? She had been here just over forty-eight hours and it wasn't the first time that Christine had heard her make such a remark. Nor had she ever, in Christine's hearing, asked him how he was. Hating the bleak tightening of Richard's mouth, she could have wept when he said with apparent amusement,

'I still have my imagination, darling.'

'And,' Pearl laughed, 'you can braille me. Isn't that what you're supposed to do?'

'If you come nearer, I'll oblige,' he murmured.

As Pearl moved over the room to him, Christine grabbed the empty log basket and fled. She had no wish to see his hands descend possessively on Pearl's shoulders.

Pearl couldn't have allowed him much time to braille either her or her dress, for a few moments later she followed Christine into the kitchen.

'Christine.' She smiled almost warmly, 'I wondered if you would mind if Richard and I dined alone this evening? I'll be leaving the day after tomorrow, so we don't have much time left to be together.'

'Of course not.' Christine didn't say that if she had her way, she wouldn't dine with them at all. It removed any pleasure she might have had out of a meal to be constantly on the receiving end of Pearl's suspicious glances. 'Just mention it to Richard.'

'We could always tell him that you have a headache.' Pearl wandered to the rusty old mirror beside the window and peered at her reflection. 'He has too much conscience.'

'Conscience?'

'I'm not sure that's the right word but he has a bee in his bonnet about the haves and have-nots in the world—always had, and I think he believes that you are one of the latter and he feels sorry for you.'

'Me?' was all Christine could think of to say.

Pearl turned to her, impatiently unflattering. 'Any stray cat! One of these days, I have a terrible feeling that he will give his money to charity and finish his days building roads and dams, offering his skills to deprived nations.'

'Would that be wrong?'

'For me it would be a disaster,' Pearl retorted bitterly.

Christine looked at her in dismay. 'You wouldn't try to stop him?'

Pearl's aloof brows rose. 'It may not come to that but if it does and I did, I don't think that I'd be committing any crime. It depends on how one looks at these things. He earns a lot of money here and he pays his taxes, which helps the poor indirectly.' Apparently satisfied that she had successfully concluded the argument, she shrugged languidly. 'Well, I'll go and tell him you aren't feeling up to dining with us.'

Christine didn't know what Pearl had told Richard but he was very offhand with her all the next day. Pearl might have been pleased with the little schemes she contrived to keep Christine out of his way, but her expression of boredom and discontent didn't change. Christine couldn't help wondering if the cosy dinner Richard and she had shared, hadn't come up to her expectations. Not that the fault might lie altogether with Pearl, she had to admit. If Pearl had been pleasanter, Christine might have felt sorry for her, for no one knew better than herself just how taciturn Richard could be.

The snow had gone during the night, leaving a depressing bleakness of drizzle and mist which shrouded the mountains and surrounding landscape. Pearl complained about not being able to get out but, as far as Christine knew, she hadn't attempted to leave the house, apart from going to church on Christmas Day. On the afternoon of Boxing Day, she seemed reduced to worrying about the possibility of the taxi not being able to get through for her the following morning.

'If it doesn't,' she told Richard, 'Christine will just have to drive me.'

'Not to Aberdeen,' he replied grimly.

'There's more snow forecast,' Pearl snapped. 'I can't risk being stuck here!'

'A few more days wouldn't hurt you.'

'It could hurt my career.'

It was difficult to tell if Richard was doubtful. Christine certainly was. Pearl must have reached the peak of her modelling career years ago and she wasn't exactly famous. If she had been younger, Christine might have believed her when she talked of being so much in demand. She was very beautiful, though, Christine had to admit that!

If Richard was thinking along the same lines, he merely murmured, 'What time's your appointment on Friday, Pearl?'

'My . . . er, oh, ten o'clock,' she said hastily, then

rushed on, 'you know how upset my agent gets if I let her down.'

'Well, don't worry,' he replied drily, 'I'll make sure you make it. After all,' he shrugged casually, 'if my eyes don't get better, we may need every penny you can earn.'

CHAPTER SIX

THAT evening, after dinner, Pearl came to the kitchen again.

Christine was as surprised to see her as she had been the night before, the kitchen not being Pearl's favourite habitat. When she pretended that she had come for a glass of water, Christine knew she had something more to say, for if the kitchen wasn't Pearl's favourite place, she usually avoided water like the plague!

Whatever Pearl had to say, however, she was in no hurry. She sat down at the table, staring at the glass of water until Christine prompted quietly, 'Where's Richard?'

'Headache,' Pearl replied briefly. He's gone to lie down for an hour.'

Christine's nerves immediately tightened with anxiety, but she only said, 'I'd better get him his tablets.'

'What tablets?'

Why did Pearl sound so startled? 'I don't know what they are, exactly, but he was warned he might get headaches. I should think, in cases like his, it's not unusual.'

'He isn't going to recover, is he? And I'm not talking about his headaches.'

Christine felt the blood drain from her face at the angry conviction in Pearl's voice. She refused to believe it herself, yet how could she argue, when she knew so little.

'What makes you think that?' she asked weakly.

Pearl looked at her, her lovely face hardening until all the beauty seemed to leave it. 'I don't happen to be stupid, Miss Colwell. Why do you think I came here for Christmas? I simply don't believe that Richard would be enduring the treatment he's having for mere eye strain. No, I'm firmly convinced that he is going blind and I've been watching him closely. He fumbles all the time and he clearly has something on his mind.'

'On his mind——'

'Don't looked so shocked,' Pearl said scornfully. 'You've been with him since the beginning, or almost, you must have noticed. He's trying to come to terms with it but I don't think he can!'

'If—if he did go blind,' Christine whispered, 'you could be of enormous help to him.'

'What about me?' Pearl snapped. 'What help would he be to me?'

'But you wouldn't need it, not in the way Richard would,' Christine murmured in bewilderment.

Pearl began pacing the floor, her long skirts swirling each time she turned. Christine watched anxiously, wondering what she was thinking. She didn't have long to wait.

'I don't think I could bear being married to a blind man,' Pearl cried suddenly. 'I need to be told I'm beautiful by a man who can see me. Otherwise, I might just as well have been born plain and ordinary.' Her eyes flickered over Christine. 'I owe it to myself, I think, not to saddle myself with a blind husband.'

Christine's eyes widened in horror. She clutched the edge of the table, Richard's tablets forgotten. 'He isn't going to be blind!' she said frantically, for Richard's sake, feeling a terrible urgency to persuade Pearl to change her mind.

'That's what you think!' Pearl retorted harshly. 'He's been having trouble with his sight for ages. I recall incidents now which I'd forgotten, most of all his blinding headaches. Last summer, he rarely stayed more than an hour at any party. Usually I had to find someone else to take me home. No one could be expected to put up with a lifetime of that.'

'Whatever you do,' Christine pleaded, 'don't do anything hasty. Give yourself time. Wait until he comes back to London. Whatever the outcome of his treatment, I'm sure, if you love him, things will work out.'

'Love!' Pearl blazed, throwing her a withering glance. 'What has that got to do with it? I've had one husband who never gave me what I wanted, I'm certainly not going to make the same mistake again!'

When she left the next day, Christine contrived to be upstairs in her room with the door closed, rather than witness the distress that Richard must be feeling over Pearl's departure. Pearl might have talked of breaking her engagement but this morning she was still wearing her ring, and the only person to have suffered a sleepless night might have been herself. Christine shivered, feeling tired because of it. It came to her painfully, that if she was responsible for Pearl having second thoughts, in the long run Richard might have nothing to thank her for. Yet if Pearl had told him she couldn't marry him, on top of what he had to endure already, what might it have done to him?

Harry came after the New Year and Christine was more than pleased to see him.

'He's been doing too much. I can't keep up with him but he won't listen!' she cried, the strain of the weeks since Christmas suddenly catching up with her, so that it all came out in a rush, almost before he was through the kitchen door, where he had obviously come looking for her.

'Hush!' Harry laughed, enveloping her in a bear-like hug. 'He's taking a phone call in the study but I can hear about him later. First, I want to know how you've been, honey. I've missed you!'

'Am I supposed to believe you?' Because he immediately lightened her heart, she laughed back. 'Pearl mentioned seeing you with a beautiful brunette.'

'Yes, well,' he grinned, 'Pearl always did talk too much. That was my sister.'

'How many sisters do you have?' She pretended to be puzzled. 'I thought you were an only child?'

'I adopt them,' he retorted.

'If you believe that, you'll believe anything,' Richard growled from the doorway.

Harry turned to him with a faintly puzzled frown on his face, though his tone was bantering. 'Don't you know when you aren't wanted, old man? Christine was just about to tell me all the things you've been up to since I was last here.'

There was a flash of impatience. 'I can save her the trouble,' Richard said shortly. 'Working, admittedly, but has she told you that she helps me—in the office, I mean? I've rarely known anyone as quick on the uptake; I never have to tell her anything twice, but she doesn't let me keep at it all day. She drags me around the loch every afternoon, I think for the pleasure of having me dependent on her, rather than for my health.'

'Richard!' she gasped, feeling wounded out of all proportion by his mildly sarcastic taunts and trying to hide it. 'You know it's for your own good.'

Harry glanced quickly from her flushed face to his cousin's hard one. 'Next time, try pushing him into the loch, Christine, it might cool him off.'

Christine was too busy wondering what had got into Richard to pay much heed to Harry's dry advice. She couldn't see his eyes but his jaw was clenched and she could sense the antagonism in rigidly flexed muscles, like some kind of violence held severely in check. It couldn't have been anything she had said, or Harry, for that matter. She had thought he would be much happier when Harry arrived, but then, hadn't she thought the same about Pearl's visit, and for all the difference it had made she may as well have stayed away.

He dismayed her further by replying to Harry indifferently, 'Christine will, no doubt, be glad to see the back of me and it shouldn't be long now.'

Christine clamped all her feelings tightly inside herself to hide them. 'I'm sure it won't be,' she said, trying to infuse a little warmth in her voice. 'Now, if you'd both like to get out of my way, I'll get on with dinner.'

Harry stayed for four days and when he left, Christine missed him. While he was there, Richard spent only the odd hour in the study and they went walking both morning and afternoon, usually with Wolf, the old mongrel dog, trailing behind them. Christine thought that Richard would have preferred going out alone with his cousin but he declared, in tones too uncompromising for flattery, that he had no intention of changing props at this late stage.

Christine was glad of the extra stocks of food they had brought from Inverness, as all the fresh air gave the two men huge appetites. These, along with her regular supplies purchased locally, enabled her to make satisfying meals.

When Harry left he insisted that he had never felt so fit in his life. 'I'm going to miss all your wonderful home cooking, my love,' he sighed, as he kissed her goodbye. 'It's been—have I said something wrong, Christine?' He frowned, as she went pale.

She recalled a time, only once, when Richard had called her that. 'No, of course not.' She forced a laugh. 'I must be overwhelmed by your appreciation.'

His eyes narrowed but he only said lightly. 'The first time you're in London, I intend trying to repay you. Right now I claim the right to take you out.'

'Harry's a flirt, don't let yourself get carried away by idle promises,' Richard remarked curtly at dinner that night.

Christine looked at him, finding it easy to sound cool when she felt frozen inside. 'If I did, would it matter? After all, we are both free and over twenty-one.'

'You've just reached it,' he retorted.

She hesitated, thinking that they might both need a moment to control themselves. Richard sounded slightly angry, while she was beginning to feel the strain of keeping all emotion clamped down. 'You don't think I take him seriously, do you?'

'Maybe not.'

He sounded faintly mollified but she gazed at him despairingly. She wondered how Pearl could even think of leaving him. He was so dear and handsome. True, he was arrogant and he had a temper, but he was so much more than any of these things that none of his faults seemed to matter.

'Is temper a sin?' she pondered aloud, without realising it.

'Depends on whose it is.' He grinned.

'Oh,' she felt a fool, 'I'm sorry . . .'

'So it was mine you were thinking about.'

Suddenly she giggled and Richard straightened his twitching lips and said severely. 'Watch it, my girl, or I might just send you packing instead of taking you with me to London.'

Christine's fork clattered on her plate. "London?' she breathed, after a moment's stunned silence.

'That's what I said.' He speared a prawn from his curry and popped it into his mouth. 'We're leaving at the end of the month.'

'Your eyes?' Having helped him through several bad nights and frequently massaged his aching shoulders, she'd had no compunction recently over mentioning his eyes. When she had first started doing so, he had balked, then to her relief, he had begun to accept it. Now, if they bothered him unduly, he usually came to her for advice. Not every time, she suspected, but then she had never expected to demolish the hard wall of his independence completely.

'I believe they will be much better.' He answered her half-formed question briefly.

She swallowed, wondering why she was getting so emotional. 'You've told Pearl?'

'We talked before she left,' he replied evasively.

He must have known something then. 'You must both be very relieved and happy,' she said huskily.

'I'll be happier when this is removed.' He tapped his blindfold derisively. 'Harry thinks I'll need spectacles for close work.'

In the excitement over his eyes, Christine had forgotten his remark about London, but, when it returned to her suddenly, he made her wait until they were having coffee in the lounge before he would explain further.

'I can't go to London with you!' she exclaimed when he firmly repeated what he had said, merely rephrasing it a little.

'What will you do, then?' he asked bluntly. 'You can't stay here.'

'Don't you still need a caretaker?' she countered helplessly.

'Yes, but not you.' The line of his mouth had a grimness which indicated that if she could see his eyes they would be hard and unrelenting. 'I won't allow myself to even consider letting you live here on your own, but you must be sufficiently aware of my thoughts on the subject not to argue.'

'I'd be all right . . .'

'Christine!'

His imperious tone silenced her but she still felt distracted. What could she do if she left Cragend? Live in a hotel until she found digs and a job? It might not be impossible but work was scarce . . .

'I'd rather go to Inverness than London,' she said.

'So you can be near Ken?'

'No,' she sighed, without anger. 'He has a girlfriend, I won't say another, because I was never that friendly with him, but if I stayed here it wouldn't be for that reason.'

If Richard appeared to relax, it was only for a second before he was saying curtly, 'If you want to get in touch with him, go out with him, before we leave, I don't mind. I realise that I've been wrong in the past. You should have friends of your own age, especially plenty of boyfriends, before you settle down.'

What had that got to do with her immediate plans? Dismissing the odd tightness in his voice, Christine declared more firmly, 'I'm not your responsibility, Richard. If you won't let me stay at Cragend, I can't make you, but I won't come to London with you. I can't, Richard . . .'

She had allowed a note of pleading to creep in, which somehow caused the elemental tension, she was coming to fear, to insert itself between them. She heard Richard's breath rasp as, ignoring her plea, he said tautly, 'You'll have to help me to get there, for one thing.'

She hadn't thought of that. 'Wouldn't Harry come for you, or Pearl?'

'It's not convenient.' In a burst of impatience, he added tersely, 'For God's sake, girl, will you stop arguing? Maybe I should have consulted you beforehand but I've come to rely on you and you've nothing else to do. Please, Christine.' He paused and said softly, 'Please say you'll do this for me?'

She had never been able to resist him when he spoke to her like that. Despising her lack of will-power, she agreed but added bleakly, 'I intend coming back.'

'Listen, Christine.' Pressing his advantage, he sat down beside her on the settee and took hold of her hand. 'Perhaps it would help if I explained what I have in mind for you once we get there.'

Her fingers stiffened in his discouragingly. 'I can't let you arrange my life.'

'No one's trying to, but I think you need help.' Straightening out her clenched fingers, he stroked them persuasively. 'Look, Christine,' he said grimly, 'you've helped me. Often I rebelled against it, but I sank my pride and let you. You can argue that I had no other choice but we both know that's not strictly true. So how about sinking your pride for a change, and letting me help you?'

'What exactly do I have to do?' she whispered, feeling suddenly shaken.

He paused, carrying her hand, seemingly idly, to his lips. Christine felt her skin tingle with darts of electricity running up her arm but she forced herself to sit still. Usually he had an instant command of persuasive language; now he seemed to be having some difficulty in finding the right words.

'In London,' he said eventually, 'you will stay with me until I find you a flat. I have a house plus a housekeeper, which should satisfy your sense of propriety, if that's what you're worrying about.'

It might seem foolish to agree with him after they had been alone together for so many weeks here. She murmured instead, 'But what shall I do?'

'There's a job for you in my office,' he informed her. 'And, before you begin to accuse me, I'm not making it up. My secretary has three assistants, one of whom has left, as she's seven months pregnant. The job can be yours until she comes back, or until you find something you like better.'

Christine felt very short of breath. She didn't know what to think. It all seemed too much, too soon. 'Won't I be doing some other girl out of a job? Someone who is more entitled to it?'

'I've trained you,' Richard snapped, as if she was questioning his judgment. 'You know my ways and though you won't have much contact with me, it will save Ida quite a few headaches.'

Ida, maybe. Christine rubbed her own aching head. What about when he was married? Even if she could find a flat, how could she go on working for him then? 'Wouldn't Pearl object?' she asked.

'Leave Pearl out of it.' He released her hand and got up again restlessly. 'You'll soon settle down, have your own flat and be quite free to entertain your own friends.'

'Will I see anything of you, once I leave your house?' she asked uncertainly, wondering why her heart should be beating so unsteadily, with the kind of despair she had never experienced before.

'I'll be in and out of the office, all being well.'

But he could be away for weeks. The whole situation

seemed to taunt her because of things left unsaid. She looked at him pleadingly, though she knew he couldn't see her. 'Why are you doing this, Richard?'

'I'll tell you why,' he replied tersely. 'You've been incarcerated here for too long. Your father had no right to isolate you in a place like this then die without leaving you a penny. That's all behind you now but until you get back into the mainstream of life you'll never be able to judge clearly what you want.'

Christine had a vague notion that she had found what she wanted in the shape of the man hovering above her. That wasn't what Richard meant though, he was speaking of jobs and criticising her father.

'Dad did his best,' she defended coldly. 'No one expects to be cut off in their forties.'

'You don't have to be that old to be able to arrange your affairs.' His mouth came together in a grim line. 'It's never been a habit of mine, raking over old ground, Christine. Any reference to your past is incidental. What interests me is your future.'

'Everything you say might be true,' she allowed, 'but I can only repeat that I'm quite old enough to look after myself, in fact, I'd rather.'

A heavy sigh came from him. 'Sometimes I'd give anything to see your face. That never lied to me.'

Between now and when he could see, she must learn to school her too-revealing features. So he couldn't detect certain things, at least.

'At the moment I'm probably looking homesick,' she tried to quip but her voice was suddenly thick and disturbed. 'I'd like to come back to Cragend, some day, Richard.'

'So would I,' he said soberly. 'I've found the kind of peace here I'd never believed in. Whether I come back or not depends.'

On Pearl, Christine thought bleakly, and as Pearl didn't like Cragend, there was little possibility of Richard coming back. If Pearl had her way, both the house and the land might soon be on the market.

During the following days, quite a few more things happened to upset Christine but most of them she managed to hide from Richard. He would merely laugh if she told him how much she would miss the view from her bedroom window, the way the first rays of morning sunshine—if there was any—glinted across the loch, how the mountains appeared sometimes to be looming over her and at other times so distant. Then there were all her wild friends, the birds, the deer, the foxes, even old Wolf; she didn't know what she was going to do without them. Yet she knew in her heart that Richard was right. There were many dear memories bound up in Cragend but she was too young to become obsessed by the past, to let it dominate her. Naturally it hurt, when it came to leaving, but she had known that it was bound to happen and she must learn to accept it. The cleaner and quicker the break perhaps the better.

The one thing she didn't succeed in hiding from Richard was her distress, when, in the late afternoon on the day before they left, while they were making their way around the loch to say goodbye to Jamie Angus, they found Wolf lying frozen in the snow. It had been snowing intermittently for days with a hard frost at night, which must have proved too much for the old, half-wild dog.

Wolf had grown frail but Christine had come to think that he was indestructible and the night before she had given him a good feed, though he had refused to sleep in the kitchen. Jamie Angus had promised to look after him when she was gone. Now she saw that he would never need a friend again.

When she first noticed him in the snow, she thought he was sleeping, but when she discovered that he was dead she turned her face against Richard with a heartbroken cry.

'What is it?' he asked urgently.

'Wolf,' she gasped between sobs.

Richard hesitated, cursing his lack of sight as Christine trembled. 'He's dead?'

'Yes.'

Drawing her gently down beside him, Richard knelt with her on the frozen ground. Though he couldn't see, he ran his hands expertly over the old dog. 'Poor old chap,' he murmured softly, confirming what Christine had told him.

'The ground's so hard,' she gulped, 'I won't be able to bury him. I'll have to ask Jamie.'

Compassionately, Richard wiped away her tears. 'At least you'll know where Wolf is.'

That night in bed, she cried again, not just for Wolf, but for everything she was saying goodbye to. The house was shrouded in dust-sheets, Jamie Angus was engaged to keep an eye on it and the finality of it all struck her afresh. Richard hadn't said anything more about his future plans but she was certain that they didn't include her. Once she was in London, safely installed in a job and digs, she doubted if she would see him again, apart from very rarely in the office.

Lying in bed, she slowly began shaking with sobs. As they grew stronger, she turned her face into the pillow to muffle any noise. She almost shot out of the bed with fright when a hand fell on her heaving shoulder.

'Christine?' Richard's voice was incredibly soft as he gathered her slight body against him, tucking her small, damp face under his chin. 'I knew you were upset about Wolf. I had to come. I couldn't bear to think of you up here all alone.'

Christine clung to him, pressing her hot face against his chest, enveloped in her own misery yet trying to control it. Every time she was in his arms she tried to remember Pearl, but the battle was usually lost before it began. What was there about Richard that so easily demolished her good intentions?

'How did you get upstairs?' she choked, ashamed of her tears as she realised the disaster they might have caused. If he had slipped!

'Quite easily,' he replied. 'Don't I keep telling you, there's nothing wrong with me, other than my eyes. I would sleep up here if I didn't think it was foolish to risk the stairs every day.'

He spoke quietly, his voice soothing as if he were trying to calm her down. Her hands trembled as she tentatively touched the taut curves of his neck, exposed by the slack cord of his robe. She tried to communicate—without putting it in words which might prove dangerous—how much she appreciated his concern.

'You should be in bed,' she said at last, when he continued to hold her tightly and didn't speak.

'I'm in bed now.'

She sighed as she felt his smile against her temple. 'You know what I mean.'

'There are still tears on your cheeks.' His lean fingers found them. 'I'll go back in a minute, once you feel better, but it's cold down there.'

Her arms tightened remorsefully. 'That's my fault, isn't it? I won't let you have a fire for fear you'll fall over it.'

'You put one on during the day.'

'That's not the same.'

'No, it isn't.' His breathing changed slightly. 'Are you all right now?'

Her head moved in an affirmative direction but he seemed as reluctant as she was to put a sensible distance between them.

'Is your nightdress cotton?' He fingered the strap closest to his hand, where it lay on her bare shoulder.

Again she nodded.

'It feels nice but you should have silks and satins.' He laughed suddenly, harshly. 'Or maybe nothing.'

She felt the disturbing difference in him, bred by the intimacy of their surroundings, not something he had planned deliberately. She could feel the warmth of his strong body, the comfort of it flowing into her, but this sudden tension seemed to snatch her breath away and heighten her senses.

She heard her brain tapping out danger signals but

she couldn't bring herself to push him away immediately. His touch, as always, had a drugging effect and his breath was warm on her cheek. She found herself enjoying the gentle exploration of his mouth as it moved over the sensitive parts of her face in a purely sensuous fashion.

When his mouth reached the corner of her lips, they turned to seek his devouring kiss of their own accord. From being warm and gently consoling, his mouth began burning with a hungry intensity. Christine's senses reeled, her heart jolted and seemed to stop, then began pounding so fiercely that her whole body was shaken by the force of it.

Then, just as she felt she was poised on the edge of some terrible precipice and intended rescuing herself, a stirring of hunger escaped her restraint and became part of her response. Within seconds it expanded, crushing all other feelings. Her arms sliding around his shoulders, she strained against him, arching to shape herself more closely to the hard angles and planes of his body.

Somehow they were lying on the bed. She could hear his heart pounding, loud and fast as he alternately caressed and moulded her slender frame to meet his needs. His hands stroked and pressed across her back, his fingers splaying her shoulder blades and delicately tracing her spine. Wherever he touched responded with a surge of such heat that she soon began thinking she was on fire.

Then, suddenly, Richard was pulling his mouth from hers, dragging air into his lungs as if they had been screaming for it, pushing her away from him, a faint tremor in his hands. As he straightened to the edge of the bed, she heard him mutter despairingly, 'What the hell am I doing?'

Christine lay stunned, unable to think, the whole day converging on her, becoming too much for her. Tonight she had found release in tears and passion, which had seemed a natural culmination of all that had happened, but Richard's abrupt rejection chilled her. She felt like a child who had been rebuffed without knowing why.

'Richard . . .?' she addressed his taut back.

'Don't say anything,' he warned.

'I was only going to thank you for being concerned about me,' she said dully, then paused. Why had he been concerned? She flushed painfully as the answer came to her in a flash. He felt sorry for her. The last thing she wanted was his pity but it was all he had to give. He shouldn't have kissed her but she hadn't been without fault herself. She had responded to him far too ardently.

Seeking to atone, to find an excuse for her own abandonment, as well as his, she murmured huskily, 'Sometimes one gets carried away by good intentions.'

Suddenly he flung himself back on the bed again, his hands behind his head. His elbows kept her at a distance but she didn't try to go near him; she felt so confused and startled.

'Go to sleep, Christine,' he said roughly. 'Stop worrying. Nothing's happened that's worth worrying about.'

'Perhaps not.' She let him think she agreed. 'I will be all right on my own, though. I'll help you downstairs.'

'I'm staying with you.'

'There's no need,' she insisted, believing he was still anxious about her.

'That's not the point,' he said patiently. 'I'm thinking of myself as much as you. I feel like staying here for a while but you'll be quite safe, I promise you, Christine. When I make love to a woman, I want to be able to see her and, anyway, you're far too innocent.'

'Innocent?'

'You are, aren't you?'

His tone told her he would tolerate nothing but the truth. 'Yes,' she admitted reluctantly.

'Go to sleep, then,' he commanded again. 'Nothing's going to hurt you.'

She didn't remember falling asleep; for a long time

she thought that she wouldn't be able to. Once, during the night, she woke to find him still lying beside her, his arms around her. She snuggled closer, oddly comforted, but in the morning, when she found herself alone, she wondered if she had dreamt it all.

On the way to London, Richard informed her that Pearl and he were no longer engaged.

Christine couldn't believe that she was hearing properly. She sat silently beside him on the plane, slightly shocked, trying to digest what he had told her, until he asked tersely if she had heard what he was saying.

She was trying to work it out. 'There was no post this morning and no one phoned.'

'What's that got to do with it?' he interrupted curtly.

'Well,' she floundered, 'how would you have known otherwise? I mean, you can't have talked to each other, as this is the first I've heard of it.'

'She decided at Christmas. She met someone else, who has apparently fallen in love with her. He has two good eyes so he can see exactly what she has to offer.'

For a moment Christine was struck dumb, her mind spinning. How could Pearl have been so cruel? That Richard hadn't said anything must imply that he had hoped she would change her mind and come back to him. Now he was returning to London again, he could no longer keep the news of his broken engagement to himself. He was having to sink his pride and tell people about it, for, after all these weeks, Pearl must be gone for good.

'This other man,' she asked carefully, 'do you know him?'

'Not personally.'

'Do you think that she will be happy with him?'

'How on earth would I know?' he retorted irritably. 'According to Pearl, he's quite wealthy and healthy, so it's probable.'

Christine sighed. Naturally he didn't wish to talk

about it. 'I'm sorry, Richard.' She was glad he couldn't see the compassionate tears in her eyes but she laid a gentle hand on his arm.

It was immediately shaken off but she persevered. 'You must feel very bad about it.' She dared not suggest that he was broken-hearted. He must be but he was too proud to admit it. 'Pearl may change her mind, you know. I think the thought of you being blind alarmed her but blindness alarms a lot of people. I'm sure her feelings can't have changed completely. Once she hears you're going to be all right, I'm certain she will come and see you.'

'If you mean, to make up,' he said bluntly, 'I wouldn't have her back at any price. I'm not heartbroken, Christine,' he added sarcastically, 'before you begin weeping all over me, I can assure you of that.'

Christine flushed, wiping her wet cheeks furtively. She didn't want to weep over him, for her tears weren't appreciated, yet she couldn't deny them. Lapsing into an unhappy silence, rather than invite another cutting remark, she tried to think sensibly about his broken engagement.

She was sad for him, dismayed that his plans for a happy, settled future had come to nothing, yet, considering what he had just said, none of this made sense. Of course he might feel that he had to pretend he didn't care that Pearl had thrown him over for another man. It wasn't an unusual attitude. What Christine didn't understand was why he hadn't told her that Pearl wasn't going to marry him until now. She frowned as she reflected, then a little anger became mixed with her commiserations. There were occasions when he had kissed her, after Christmas, when he must have known the response she felt made her feel guilty about Pearl. Though she didn't believe he had ever planned to kiss her, couldn't he easily have told her the truth?

Christine was tense, staring at Richard, for once not concerned that he might sense she was doing it. Had he believed that, if he told her the truth, she might read more than he intended into a few casual kisses? Had he thought that she might make a nuisance of herself if she knew he was no longer engaged? Or had he kissed her, encouraged her to fall in love with him a little, merely as a form of revenge against women in general, because of the way Pearl had treated him?

Suddenly she remembered that Pearl had still been wearing her engagement ring when she left, but when Christine remarked on this to Richard, he merely snapped,

'Because I told her she could keep it. She did ask if I wanted it back but what would I want with it? I certainly have no intention of putting my head in a similar noose again.'

CHAPTER SEVEN

HARRY met them in London. Before they landed, Richard said, 'When we arrive, I'm going straight to the clinic with Harry. I'm not sure how long I'll be there.'

'Am I coming with you?' Christine asked.

'God no!' He sounded as if that might just about finish him off. He smiled slightly, as if to soften the impact of his words. 'You'll stay at my house, it's already arranged. Mrs Webster will look after you, she's expecting you, and tomorrow, if I'm not home, she'll ring for a taxi to take you to the office. Ida Wright will find you something to do. I spoke to her from Cragend.'

With foolish desperation, Christine had hoped that she might be allowed to wait for him at the clinic. 'Have you any idea when you will be home?' she whispered, more concerned for him than for herself. Leaving Cragend had proved more daunting than she'd anticipated. She had almost disgraced herself by breaking down. Nearing London, the transition from lonely isolation in the Highlands to the noise and bustle of a capital city had struck her even more forcibly, making her feel slightly sick. Yet all the trauma she experienced was nothing compared to the anxiety she knew over Richard. She could be furious with him, despise him, but she only had to think of him having to endure something that might hurt him, for anxiety to cancel out all those other feelings.

She saw him shake his head to her query. 'You will take care?' she murmured helplessly.

His mouth twisted wryly. 'I'm going to make sure this damned bandage is removed, whatever happens. Otherwise I'm not likely to be doing anything you wouldn't approve of.'

'You will be able to see.'

It wasn't a question. She spoke fiercely, as if she felt it imperative to convince him.

Again his mouth moved derisively. 'I'm not blind, Christine, which is what a lot of people, including yourself and my former fiancée appear to believe. There's some controversy over it but I'm convinced that I hurt my eyes in an accident. Harry isn't so sure—he still thinks it's some kind of strain. If this treatment hasn't cured whatever it is, and impaired sight is something I have to learn to live with, I may find it hard but I won't complain. Whatever happens, as I've told you before, I'm not an invalid.'

Christine liked Richard's house. After the taxi which had taken him and Harry to the clinic dropped her off on his doorstep, she stood gazing at it for a minute before she rang the bell.

It was an imposing house, in an area she recognised as expensive. Her father's house in Kensington had been nice but nothing like this.

She liked Mrs Webster, Richard's housekeeper, too. She was a pleasant, middle-aged woman and, though apt to treat her like a deprived child, she was very kind.

'You're the young lady who has been working for him in Scotland.' She smiled as she showed Christine to her room. 'You're going to be working for him here as well, he says.'

As Christine nodded, she laughed. 'How did he get on with the housekeeper up there? I expect he led her quite a dance, along with the rest of the staff. He wasn't the easiest man to get on with when he could see. I was glad I didn't have the job of looking after him while he couldn't. I've been praying, though, that he's going to be all right. The house hasn't been the same without him, I can tell you.'

'I'm sure it hasn't been,' Christine murmured, dropping her suitcase gently on the beautiful pink carpet.

Mrs Webster fussily adjusted the chintz curtains. 'It will be nice to have someone young about the place again, I must say, but Mr Richard tells me you're looking for a flat. Young people like to be independent, nowadays.'

Mrs Webster, Christine soon learned, seldom waited for an answer to her own questions. She usually answered them herself, which was perhaps just as well. She didn't know if Richard had been saving her from possible embarrassment, so she didn't mention that, at Cragend, she had been housekeeper, staff and secretary combined.

'If you'd like to come down to the lounge, Miss, as soon as you're ready, I'll bring you a nice cup of tea.' Mrs Webster smiled. 'Mr Richard said I was to, as soon as you arrived.'

Christine felt warmed by Richard's thoughtfulness, until she remembered that that was the pattern by which he lived. He was extremely methodical in all he did. She had noticed his assiduous attention to detail at Cragend. It was second nature to him, part of his general competence. Her tea would have been ordered without any particular interest in her welfare. In his opinion, she was someone in need of assistance and to be dealt with as such. The romantic illusions, the emotional tension was all on her side; to imagine that he would look at her twice, now that he was back in London, was perhaps the greatest illusion of them all.

'Mr Kingsley has a beautiful home,' she remarked to Mrs Webster, as she carried her tea-tray back to the kitchen. The kitchen was an ultra-modern department and, apart from being large, in no way resembled the one at Cragend. She swallowed as she was reminded of how empty the one there would be, with only the ghost of old Wolf to haunt it, and quickly thought of something else.

'This is all very nice,' Mrs Webster sniffed, as Christine's eyes widened on all the chrome and gleaming tiles. 'But what a house needs is a mistress.

Mind you, I don't know that I'll stay on, once Mr Richard is married to Mrs Kristol.'

Didn't Mrs Webster know of his broken engagement? Christine frowned, deciding that she couldn't, but also deciding that it was none of her business and that Richard must tell her himself.

Gently she tried to change the subject. 'I used to live in London. I was actually born here. Now I'm not at all sure I can find my way around.'

Mrs Webster was unwittingly distracted from her dubiousness over her employer's forthcoming marriage. She immediately wanted to know how long it was since Christine had lived here and when Christine told her, she laughed. 'Oh, it will soon all come back. In no time, you'll feel you've never been away. A few years is nothing.'

When Christine made the mistake of saying that she had become used to Scotland, Mrs Webster returned to Richard again, like a homing pigeon. 'Mr Richard didn't want to go, I could tell, but he got to like it so much he didn't want to leave. What I couldn't understand was why his fiancée didn't go with him. I know she went to see him but that's not the same thing, is it?'

'She has her work,' Christine murmured evasively.

'You must have met her,' Mrs Webster said sharply. 'What did you think of her?'

Christine frowned. Mrs Webster shouldn't be asking her opinion. She must realise that but she was clearly too anxious over Richard's engagement to be discreet. Christine wished he had told her that he was no longer engaged, though the fact that he hadn't seemed to confirm her former suspicions that, despite what he had said, he was hoping that Pearl would come back to him again. 'I didn't get to know Mrs Kristol very well, I'm afraid,' she replied awkwardly.

'Been married before, you know,' Mrs Webster muttered. 'Nothing wrong with that, except that I don't think she's right for him. Too high-falutin', for one thing!'

The prospect of Pearl becoming part of the household was clearly preying on Mrs Webster's mind but Christine knew she couldn't discuss Pearl with her. For one thing, when she learned that Richard and Pearl had split up, if she suspected that Christine had known all along, she might never forgive her. This might not be important, as Christine knew she would soon be living elsewhere and might not see her again, but she had no wish to hurt anyone, even someone she scarcely knew.

Her immediate dilemma was resolved, however, when a tradesman called. Christine excused herself as Mrs Webster spoke to him, and returned to her room.

She unpacked reluctantly, wishing she had gone to a hotel. Richard couldn't have stopped her and she could have afforded to. He had paid her generously for looking after him in Scotland but she must stop obeying him so blindly. She couldn't become entirely reliant on him, or she would never learn to manage on her own. And that was something she was determined to do as soon as possible.

As she folded her shabby clothes into huge drawers which seemed to mock their inadequacy, she sighed. She was sensible enough to realise that she couldn't do without some help at this stage. By swallowing her pride, she would find it much easier to get settled in London. If she could get through the next few weeks she might be confident enough to get through anything. Once she found somewhere to live, she would begin looking for another job, so that she could leave Richard's employment immediately. To begin with, he might be annoyed but once he was absorbed in his normal routine again, he would probably never notice she was gone.

The following morning, as Richard had promised, a taxi arrived to take her to his office. Miss Wright was as pleasant as Mrs Webster but whereas the latter was motherly and bustling, Richard's secretary gave the instant impression of briskness and self-sufficiency.

As Christine walked in, she looked slightly puzzled,

then she looked closer and her face mysteriously cleared. Christine felt she had been weighed up and not found entirely wanting, though she believed someone as astute as Miss Wright would reserve judgment until she knew her better.

'I was expecting you.' She smiled as Christine hastily introduced herself. 'Mr Kingsley said you would be coming. If you hang your coat through that door, over there, I'll show you where to begin.'

She had a lot of material waiting to be typed. It looked straightforward enough but Christine wondered whether Richard had mentioned just how much orthodox training she'd had. She managed adequately and was beginning to feel quite satisfied with her skills until she had time to look around properly and noticed a desk at the other side of the large outer office equipped with a computer and word processor. Her heart sank. Whether here, or elsewhere, what would she do if she was called upon to operate something like that?

Miss Wright appeared to be quite pleased with what she had completed by lunch time. 'I usually have two assistants, three when necessary, but Richard probably told you that Mrs Jordan took leave to have a baby. My other one, Wendy Millar, has either flu or a severe cold. I didn't bother to replace her as I knew you were coming and, with Richard away, we aren't all that busy.'

Christine had wondered about the other girls and she felt better now that she knew. She had begun to believe that Richard had made them up, along with a job for her.

Miss Wright said she was to have lunch with her. 'Richard's orders.' She smiled. 'Your first day. When Wendy returns, you'd probably prefer to go with her as you're about the same age.'

'Do you think you will be able to settle?' she asked when they were sitting in a comfortable restaurant, eating salads. 'I hope you're going to like being with us.'

Christine glanced up warily. Miss Wright wasn't a dragon or anything like it, but again Christine wondered how much Richard had told her. Instinct warned her to be cautious.

'Isn't it more a case,' she said wryly, 'of discovering whether I'm suitable? And whether you are going to like me?'

'Oh, I can almost assure you of that,' Miss Wright said approvingly. 'I'll admit I prefer to choose my own assistants, simply because I have to work with them, but Richard does know what I like. He should do.' She smiled. 'I worked for his father. I've been with the firm now for twenty-five years.'

Christine was impressed. She gazed at Miss Wright in awe. 'Twenty-five years working for Richard!'

'No,' Miss Wright laughed, shaking her grey head. 'Only ten years working for him. He's not that old.'

'No, of course not.' Christine flushed. 'I wasn't thinking. I've never worked for a large firm,' she went on quickly, to hide her embarrassment. What would Miss Wright say if she confessed that she had only worked for her father?

'Well, Richard's business is big enough,' Miss Wright declared, a note of pride in her voice, 'and you won't get any better. Of course he is a brilliant engineer. That is why we were all so shocked about his eyes.'

Christine prayed that Miss Wright wouldn't mention his engagement but though she may have been curious, she had more discretion than Mrs Webster. She didn't ask any questions about why Christine was staying with him either, for which Christine was grateful. She talked only of more general things until it was time to return to the office.

By five-thirty, Christine wasn't exhausted but she was decidedly tense. The day had seemed long. Sometimes she'd closed her eyes and wished that, when she opened them, she could see the loch through the windows and the mountains beyond. The tall buildings opposite disturbed her; she wondered if she would ever get used to them and she worried all the time about Richard; what were they doing to him? She hadn't been able to ring him, as she didn't know the name of the clinic.

When she returned to his house that evening, and found he was back, she could have screamed with relief. She didn't even mind what he could read in her eyes, for his were no longer concealed and he could obviously see clearly. She had to restrain herself from throwing her arms around him and hugging him.

'Richard!' she exclaimed huskily, unable to keep all the emotion out of her voice. 'How are you?'

'Fine,' he replied, non-committally, as she burst into the lounge when Mrs Webster told her where he was. 'I have to wear glasses for close work and take care, that's all.'

'I'm so glad.' She tempered a more fervent exclamation. 'What do you mean by taking care?'

'Just that,' he retorted, with an irritability that warned her not to persist.

She would ask Harry. Richard might ignore any instructions he received, unless someone else knew about them and nagged him into carrying them out.

It was strange to be able to look into his eyes again. She had forgotten how green they were. She felt her heart beating unevenly, as he seemed just as curious about her eyes. For a moment, she thought he was going to kiss her but the moment passed. His eyes darkened and a muscle jerked at the corner of his mouth but that was all. Stepping away from her, he said sardonically, 'I think I've heard enough about eyes to last me a lifetime. How about telling me about your first day at the office?'

It wasn't easy to talk about herself, when she was only interested in what had been happening to him but every time she edged the conversation towards him, he adroitly began talking about something else.

It was the same during dinner and over coffee afterwards. He steered clear of anything personal, keeping her amused with brief stories of his foreign travels, laced with dry anecdotes about the various colourful characters he had met. It sounded friendly enough, she thought, suddenly despairing, so why did she feel convinced that he was deliberately putting distance between them again?

She was startled when, in the middle of describing a street fight in Hong Kong, he paused abruptly and said curtly, 'You will need new clothes. Take tomorrow morning off and go shopping.'

He had asked how she liked working for his firm, as Miss Wright had, but, unlike her, he had made it sound more like a polite enquiry. He had listened to what she had to say without noticeable interest. It puzzled Christine that he seemed much more concerned that she appeared to need some new clothes.

'I don't have to rush out and buy some straight away, do I?' she objected. 'I know I didn't bother much at Cragend but clothes weren't so important there.'

'They are important anywhere,' he retorted. 'Another mistake your father made, letting you run around like an urchin. I have noticed,' he continued, ignoring the indignation in her eyes, 'that you have good dress sense. The few things you've got, suit you, so you should have no difficulty in getting together a wardrobe more suitable for London. You don't have to be extravagant. You also need a good hairdresser.' His glance narrowed over her small, perfectly shaped head, over which curls rioted in glorious but unrestrained abundance. 'I've made an appointment for you. I'll pay for everything, of course.'

Really agitated now, Christine jumped to her feet. He was carrying on exactly as he had done at Cragend, while the situation here was entirely different.

'Richard!' she exclaimed, meeting his glinting green eyes bravely. 'You know I can't let you pay for things like that. There's no need, anyway. I haven't spent a penny of what you paid me in Scotland and you must allow me to be independent. I don't even like staying here for nothing. I wouldn't, if I didn't know that it was only for a few days, but I do draw the line at clothes and things.'

His eyes glittered even more and his mouth tightened. 'You will do as I say!'

'No!' Christine retorted, just as determinedly. 'It reminds me too much of a fairy-tale. Girl comes to big city and someone waves a magic wand, trying to turn an ugly duckling into a beautiful swan . . .'

He smiled coldly. 'You aren't talking sense, Christine, but I'll forgive you.' Coming to her side, he placed his fingers under her chin and raised it. 'Don't under-estimate yourself, my dear. You are small and slender with an enchanting face. If I were entirely selfish——' He broke off roughly.

'Yes?' she breathed as his teeth snapped abruptly and she became aware of the building tension between them.

'Never mind.' Releasing her, he stepped away from her tersely. 'Let's stick to what we were discussing originally. You have to learn to appreciate nice things and to enjoy yourself. When I return to the office, I intend to ask Miss Wright to arrange an informal get-together so that you can meet everyone.'

She frowned, conscious of his watching eyes and calmly folded arms. He looked relaxed but his eyes were hard, filled with what she could only think of as some kind of resolve. 'I've nothing against parties,' she murmured, 'but why is it neccessary for me to meet your staff?'

'So you can get to know people of your own age.' His voice grated with impatience. 'At Cragend there were only old people, apart from Granger.'

'I had plenty of friends.'

'There were a lot of people you said hello to, which isn't the same thing. Christine,' hard colour edged under his cheekbones as his hands clamped suddenly on her shoulders, 'how could you judge the depth of your feelings, for instance, when your experience is so limited?'

She flushed, biting her lip, conscious of shafts of fire

from his hands, shooting right through her. He was examining her small expressive features, wide blue eyes and quivering mouth, like a man filling himself with the sight of something of which he has been deprived for far too long. Her heart tripped against her rib cage in disturbing reaction.

'You disapproved of Ken,' she gasped.

'He wasn't suitable.'

What did he consider suitable? 'Ken went to university and his father owns factories.'

'Still fretting for him, are you, despite the new girlfriend?'

'No.' She gazed at him mutinously. 'I do miss Scotland though. I may go back.'

'You won't, at least not yet.' One of his hands moved upwards, caressing her neck until a sweet, tormenting misery welled in her throat, choking off the sharp reply she was about to make. Bending his head, as if he couldn't stop himself, he took her lips in a slow, heady kiss, dragging a response from her which she tried to withhold. She couldn't. She found herself returning the fierce sensual pressure of his mouth against hers. The wild intensity of her pleasure bordered on pain but she managed to suppress most of her longing.

Lightly his hands sought her breasts, contacting flesh which responded to such exciting stimulus. Her pulses rocketing, she shifted nearer, until she became conscious of the solid outline of his muscular thighs pressing on her legs and the heat of his body burning through her clothes.

She drew back with choked breath and he let her go, whipping around to the fireplace so that she wouldn't see his face, but what he said chilled her.

'We know that you're capable of the right responses, at least. I'm sure you won't be the social disaster you anticipate.'

'No,' she agreed dully, briefly hating him, with feelings so intense that it was imperative to get away from him. 'I have to have my own place.'

'You can move in next week.' He turned back to her brusquely, his face a mask again.

He eyes widened incredulously. 'I haven't looked for anything yet . . .'

'It's all arranged.' He ran a hand impassively over his crisp black hair. Without giving her a chance to reply, he added, 'I have some business to attend to in my study, Christine, so I'll say good night. Perhaps you'd like to amuse yourself watching TV? According to Mrs Webster, there's a good film on.'

Christine didn't watch the film. Instead she found a book and went to bed. If she could have found enough courage she might have followed Richard, but the solid mahogany doors of his study here seemed even less approachable than those at Cragend. There were questions she wanted to ask him, especially regarding his eyes. There were things she considered she had some right to know but he had persisted in talking about his foreign travels and her clothes. She didn't know why, she hadn't even any idea, why he had kissed her. What was the use of caring for a man who was such an enigma? She felt hurt and shut out, with all sorts of unsettling things rushing through her mind. She would have to wait until she saw Harry before she discovered whether Richard was really as well as he declared himself to be, but as she had no idea when that would be, she didn't find it very comforting.

Next morning she was awakened by the sound of heavy rain against her bedroom window. It made her wish that she could turn over and go back to sleep. Rain in the country wasn't always unpleasant, in town it usually was. She blamed this for feeling depressed until she remembered how Richard had lectured her the evening before about a shopping trip.

She tried to weigh up the pros and cons of going shopping. Richard couldn't actually force her into doing anything. Only—she wriggled her toes wryly against the satin sheets—if she didn't do as he commanded. he might make the next few days very uncomfortable for her.

Trying to convince herself that it might be better to humour him for peace, she had a quick shower and dressed. Richard was already in the dining-room when she got downstairs.

'Good morning.' She smiled. 'I'll go and see if I can help Mrs Webster.'

'You will do no such thing,' he said firmly. 'You aren't a maid and I won't have you acting like one. Besides, Mrs Webster wouldn't like it.'

Christine despised herself for giving in to him but it didn't seem worthwhile to argue. She tried not to glance at him again, already having a clear picture of how he looked imprinted on her mind. This morning, he was wearing a dark blue suit with a white shirt which emphasised the dark cast of his face and, for no reason she could think of, made her pulses race. Everything about him was immaculate. Her eyes fastened on his wrists which was a mistake, for under pristine cuffs and a thin gold watch, the coating of fine dark hairs on his skin almost took her breath away.

What was the matter with her? She was reacting like a teenager who had never seen a man before. Granted, Richard was tall and well-made but he wasn't conventionally good-looking. His face was too hard, his features too forcible, to allow him to be strictly handsome. He might make heads turn but that was his arrogance, his air of imperious authority, she told herself disparagingly.

She didn't realise she was trying to set up barriers against him, but she was aware that he spelled some kind of danger she had to fight. His image stamped itself on her senses no matter how hard she tried to resist. Her blue eyes dilated as she stared at him and she lowered them swiftly, frightened of what they might reveal. Last night he had kissed her and she'd been lost in a mindless blur of sensation, but he had never betrayed that she in any way affected him.

'Coffee, Christine?' He poured it out and she accepted with a confused word of thanks.

'I didn't realise it was in.'

'I know you didn't,' he spoke with surprising gentleness.

'Richard . . .?'

'Yes?'

'Oh, it doesn't matter.' She had been going to take advantage of his softer mood but even as she glanced at him his face hardened again. 'Well, I wondered,' she floundered, on a rash spurt of courage, 'would you mind if I left my shopping until the weekend? Yesterday was my first day in your office and Miss Wright isn't going to be pleased if I don't turn up, especially when her other girl's off. Wendy Millar has the flu.'

While she waited, positively holding her breath, she thought he was about to relent, but if she was right, apparently he changed his mind.

'Miss Wright and I will be in conference all morning so there wouldn't be much point in you being there, anyway. Carry on as planned and I'll pick you up outside Harrods at one-thirty. Don't be late; I don't want a ticket for illegal loitering.'

She wasn't late. Some time during the morning she had stopped simmering with resentment and longing to defy him. She was waiting on the pavement complete with arms full of parcels, as he drew up beside her.

'Get in,' he said, opening the door without getting out. 'I'm hungry.'

'So am I.' She smiled as he reminded her of the Richard who had often come into the kitchen at Cragend. Launching herself into the seat beside him, she threw her packages in the back. 'Apart from getting my hair done, I've never stopped all morning.'

'Women!' he jeered, slanting a mocking eye at her parcels.

'It was your idea,' she muttered, 'I hope you're satisfied—I spent nearly all of my money.'

He hadn't been able to see her behind all the things

she was carrying but now that he could, she heard him draw a sharp breath as his eyes went swiftly over her and he told her that she looked good.

'That doesn't do you justice,' he muttered, shooting off down the street as if suddenly realising where he was. 'You look quite different, what did they do to you?'

He sounded as if he hadn't wanted her changed that much and Christine was sure, that he would discover she wasn't—when he had time to take a good look at her. Yet she didn't like the tense line of his jaw. She removed her eyes from it and watched the traffic as he was forced to reduce his speed.

'I don't think anyone did anything to me,' she said eventually. 'I'm wearing a new coat and dress and they showed me how to use make-up properly, where I had my hair done or,' she laughed, 'perhaps I should say expertly. A little surface gloss, that's all.'

'All!' he muttered under his breath, parking near a restaurant in Brompton Road. 'Let's get inside before I have an accident through not keeping my eyes where they should be.'

'This is a new Italian restaurant,' he said, when they were seated. 'There seems to be a pasta plague in the land and most young people like it. I'm not sure I'm terribly enthusiastic myself, but I can thoroughly recommend the *spaghetti alle vongole*. If it hasn't gone off since I was last here.'

There he was again, speaking as if she was a schoolgirl sister he was treating. She glanced at the profusion of marble columns and original achitecture. 'It's certainly glamorous and amusing.'

'Spaghetti post-modernism,' he grunted. 'Doesn't it appeal to you?'

'It's fun and different, but you didn't have to put something on for me specifically.' Her blue eyes sparkled across the table at him. 'How am I going to work full of pasta? Yesterday, Miss Wright and I had salads.'

'Rabbit meat,' he dismissed. 'Though I confess to liking it with steaks.'

'They're good for you,' Christine said and was rewarded with an unimpressed glance.

After ordering what sounded like a gargantuan meal, he turned his attention to her again, his eyes going over her even more closely than before. 'I should have left you as you were,' he said bleakly. 'Now I'll have half my staff after you.'

She flushed. 'Don't be silly, I'm quite ordinary. A few clothes don't make that much difference.'

'Maybe not,' he retorted. 'Perhaps you were like a diamond, though a diamond's too hard for you—just in need of a little polishing and a new setting. You were always pretty, now you are beautiful.'

'Richard,' she whispered, as his eyes darkened to near black and her traitorous pulses were racing before she could control them. At last she was able to replace the tremor in her voice with a hint of mockery. 'You're talking nonsense.'

'I'm not.' His expression dared her to continue arguing with him. 'You are very desirable.'

Deliberately she murmured. 'You aren't looking for a substitute for Pearl? Someone to amuse you until you find someone else?'

His mouth tightened. 'One of these days, my girl, I'm going to lay you over my knee. I've had an urge to do so several times, so don't push your luck too far, you may need it.'

'I said the wrong thing?'

He still looked at her severely. 'Instead of pretending you don't know what he's on about when a man pays you a compliment, try saying thank you for a change. As for Pearl, I don't want to talk about her. Haven't I already told you, that it's all finished.'

She would feel better if she could believe him. They ate their pasta in silence, the wine which came with it cool against their throats. The silence wasn't uncomfortable, just full of things left unsaid.

Eventually Richard asked, 'How are you finding London?'

Emerging from the dark muddle of her thoughts, Christine smiled wryly. 'Fine, it's all coming back. It's funny, but suddenly, while I was shopping, I began to feel that I'd never been away. Streets, short cuts, special shops; I knew where I was, everywhere. I began feeling like a Londoner again.'

Richard's glance pierced and sharpened. 'You think you're going to love it again?'

She hesitated, looking at him steadily. 'Love could be too strong a word. I do feel some affinity but not that much. Being born here must make a difference but I think I'll always prefer the country.'

'You can't be sure though.'

She shrugged as his brows rose. 'I realise a lot of people buy a house in the country, thinking they'll love it, then can't wait to get back to town. Often they don't give it a fair trial, the way Dad and I did. I lived at Cragend for several years, so I consider I'm able to judge, perhaps better than most, where I'd really like to live.'

'It would have to be Cragend, though?'

'No, not necessarily.' She wasn't sure what he was getting at. 'When I left Cragend, I might have said so, but after only three days away from it, I'm not so sure. It must be nice,' she said suddenly, with a teasing smile, 'to be like you, able to afford several homes so you can go wherever the mood takes you.'

'A choice of residences, eh, Christine?' He placed his hand over hers on the table, his thumb rubbing hers, lightly caressing. 'I can assure you that owning a house in every country in the world wouldn't be much use unless one had the right person with whom to share it.'

'You aren't setting up another proposal are you, old chap?' a mocking voice interrupted sardonically.

Christine's startled eyes flew upwards to meet Harry's laughing ones. Richard didn't seem very pleased to see him but he didn't look as embarrassed as Christine, as she snatched her hand from under his.

'What the hell are you doing here?' he asked his cousin, with mild impatience. 'You're worse than a cork.'

Harry clearly had no sense of being insulted or unwelcome. He sat down beside them, uninvited and quite unperturbed. 'You forget that I was there when that delicious nurse recommended this place. I enjoy Italian food, so I thought I'd have a stab at it. Unfortunately,' his eyes rested unmistakably on Christine, 'when I rang a certain young lady, thinking that she would be available to accompany me, I was told she was working.'

CHAPTER EIGHT

RICHARD looked at him sceptically. 'Was there no other beautiful girl available?'

'No one willing to come with me.'

'That will be the day,' Richard retorted sarcastically.

'No, well,' Harry admitted with a grin, 'truth to tell, I was so disappointed that Christine couldn't come, I just couldn't endure the thought of anyone else. I decided to lunch alone.'

'My heart weeps for you,' said Richard unfeelingly. 'And you can't join us, we're just leaving.'

'And I thought my luck had changed,' Harry muttered gloomily, still looking at Christine. 'If you get any lovelier, honey, I'm going to be falling in love with you. I think I'm halfway there already.'

'Christine and I are in a hurry.' Richard pulled her to her feet, ignoring Harry's remark with a dark look. 'See you around sometime.'

'Harry!' Christine found her voice when it was almost too late. 'I'd like to have lunch with you.'

'Tomorrow?'

'She'll be too busy,' Richard snapped; then relented with such obvious reluctance that Christine couldn't help wondering why. 'I suppose,' he sighed tersely, 'she has to eat.'

'I'll pick you up at Ric's office, one o'clock sharp,' Harry said quickly, before Richard could change his mind.

She nodded as she was dragged away.

'If I go on eating like this, I'll soon need more clothes,' she grumbled, getting into Richard's car again. 'In a bigger size!'

'You didn't have to accept.'

'I——' She had been going to say that she had to talk

to Harry about him but something warned her he wouldn't like it, so she rephrased. 'I felt it was the least I could do when he's been so kind and you were so abrupt.'

'So,' he muttered cynically, 'I dig my own grave.'

'What?'

'Nothing. Would you like to see your new flat?'

She had insisted on having one but it seemed as if he couldn't wait to be rid of her. She glanced at him unhappily. 'I thought I wasn't getting it until next week?'

'You aren't but I can show it to you.'

'Do you have time?'

'We are taking the afternoon off.'

She tried not to hear the satisfied note in his voice. It had often been there in Scotland when he'd considered he was one up on her.

'It would be all day for me,' she said anxiously. 'Miss Wright isn't going to like it.'

'Leave her to me.'

'But is it fair?' Christine persisted. 'Richard,' she turned to him appealingly, 'I don't want to play at working. No one will take me seriously if I do. Miss Wright was very tolerant with me yesterday and I wouldn't like her to think I was taking advantage of her good nature. It wouldn't do me any good, either,' she finished drily, thinking of the comments there would be if she skipped work every time Richard lifted his little finger. In no time at all she would be cast as his girlfriend or even worse.

Grim and restless, he swung his gaze away from her, flicking it over the crowded streets, flashing it back to her. 'You're right,' he admitted tautly. And, as if he had read her thoughts, 'It would only invite gossip, which we can do without.'

'Thank you,' she whispered.

'I'm finding it difficult to settle after Scotland,' he confessed.

So he missed it. Her heart warmed a little. 'You

worked there, though, remember. Too hard, considering . . .'

'I had my reasons. They hadn't all to do with business.'

She didn't think they had been. There would be his eyes and his broken engagement for another thing. Even now, though he insisted that he didn't miss Pearl, he must do.

'Well, back to the grind.' He shrugged, changing direction. 'I can always take you to see your flat on our way home.'

In the underground car park below the offices, he began packing her parcels into the boot of his car.

'Won't they be all right where they are?' Christine protested.

'I'm laying them flat for you,' he said coolly, with an upwards glance. 'Unless you want to spend the evening pressing out creases?'

She would rather spend it in his arms. She flushed as she thrust the unbidden thought away from her, biting on the softness of her lower lip as she remembered his wandering mouth. A lot of good such thoughts did her!

'They wouldn't have taken any harm,' she heard herself reiterating like a parrot.

'Stop arguing, Christine.'

She looked at him furtively as they shot up in the lift to his floor. What had happened to them since they'd left Scotland? She felt uncertain of everything, while Richard, who had probably never felt uncertain in his life, appeared to have something bothering him. Ordinarily, she was sure that he would never have given her shopping a second glance, let alone have fussed over it.

Miss Wright looked up with a smile as they entered her office and didn't seem at all put out when Richard didn't return it. He disappeared through another door after asking Christine if she was sure everything was to her liking. She wished he hadn't asked, as she caught the enigmatic expression on his secretary's face.

Normally, she guessed, he never showed concern for a mere typist, unless she was ill. All of which seemed to confirm her former impression that something was bothering him.

After that, she was relieved when he appeared to forget her and the afternoon flew by. Miss Wright liked her new dress and hairstyle and had no fault to find with her work. Most of the afternoon she was on her own, as Miss Wright was kept occupied by Richard. She was surprised to discover it was six o'clock when he told her abruptly that it was time to go.

'Ida thinks that in a few weeks you'll be wasted here,' he said as they got into his car. 'She thinks you could easily be destined for higher things, if you applied yourself.'

'You've been discussing me.'

'No,' he retorted. 'It was just a comment Ida occasionally makes about a new girl. I don't usually listen.'

'Sorry,' she murmured.

'Have you ever thought seriously about the future, Christine? What you really want to do? It's a pity you didn't go on to university after leaving boarding school.'

Christine could think of one thing that she would like to be, which wouldn't be possible. 'I could still go to university, I suppose, or take evening classes. During the next few weeks I'll think about it.'

'Good.'

Why did he sound so terse? She sighed and asked, 'Where is this flat, exactly?'

'We are there now.'

They drew up outside a large modern building, a mile or so from where Richard lived. It looked expensive. He spoke to the commissionaire, then they went up to the top floor in one of the lifts.

'Here we are.' He checked the number and opened the door, stepping aside to allow her to precede him into the apartment.

There was a hall, kitchenette, living-room and a bedroom, all beautifully furnished. After Cragend and Richard's house, it seemed very small but it was all she needed. After looking at everything, she went to the window. Even the view was nice, with trees and gardens.

'Won't it be more than I can afford?' Doubtfully she turned back to Richard.

'I shouldn't think so,' he said.

'I've heard of the astronomical rents in London.' She frowned suddenly. 'How did you happen to have a key, by the way? Who is the landlord?'

'I am.'

'You?' Her eyes widened indignantly. 'You might have said.'

'You didn't ask,' he replied mildly. 'Anyway, what difference can it make?'

'None,' she admitted, 'so far as that goes, but I don't want any favours.'

'You aren't getting any,' he almost snapped. 'You won't find the rent easy to pay out of your present salary but you might look for months before you found anything else.'

'There must be people queuing up for a place like this.'

'Listen.' Richard looked as if he would like to shake her. 'Would you think twice about accepting a favour, as you call it, from Harry, or your friend Granger? It's either this or stay where you are.'

'You mean, with you?'

'Yes.'

How uncompromising he was. 'I can't,' she whispered, knowing the strain of it might kill her. Working for Richard until she found another job was bad enough, to continue living with him was impossible.

Her reply appeared to light a flame of anger in the eyes of the man watching her. 'Can't wait to get away from me, can you?'

Colour crept into her cheeks but she lifted her chin bravely. 'I stayed with you in Scotland.'

'And hated it.'

'No.'

'Liar,' he said softly.

'Well,' she sucked in a shaky breath, 'you weren't always easy to get on with, but that's not the point. You must be aware that it will only cause talk if I stay with you here.'

'With Mrs Webster as chaperone?'

'All right.' She gave in to his raised eyebrows. 'Maybe there wouldn't be talk, but it wouldn't work out. I can't have someone helping me all the time. I have to learn to stand on my own feet.'

'I know.' To her relief, he appeared to believe her. 'It's important to you.'

'Couldn't I have the flat tomorrow?' she asked, wandering to a cupboard and opening the door without looking in.

'The electric wiring is being checked,' he muttered absently. 'Along with a few other things. You can move in next Wednesday.'

Which meant another week. Seven more days alone with him, at the mercy of feelings she found daily harder to fight. When she saw Harry tomorrow, he might be able to advise her what to do, but how much could she tell him without giving herself away? Even the flat, which had seemed the answer to everything, might present new problems, because Richard owned it.

Richard hadn't seemed very happy about her lunching with Harry but he made no further mention of it until they were having breakfast the following morning.

'Don't let my cousin turn your head,' he said abruptly, as she poured him a second cup of coffee. 'Women are always susceptible to good-looking doctors.'

Christine smiled to herself bitterly, wishing she had

met Harry before him. 'There might be worse fates,' she taunted lightly.

'I'm warning you.' His green eyes glittered dangerously. 'You haven't any experience of men like him.'

A demon of a type she didn't recognise, drove her on. 'There's only one way of getting it.'

'Christine!'

Feeling slightly ashamed of herself, she backed down. 'I don't think Harry is particularly dangerous.'

'You don't know what sexual danger is,' he said derisively. 'You've never been exposed to it.'

Hadn't she? A betraying pulse jerked in her throat as her thoughts flew to Cragend and the night Richard had slept with her. She had experienced a thousand emotions then, walking a tightrope between overwhelming passion and sanity. That sanity had won might have had more to do with Richard than herself but she was certain there had been more than an element of danger in it. Richard might deny all knowledge of it but even last night, when he had kissed her, she had sensed she was in some kind of jeopardy. Men must be all the same; that was why they were so suspicious of each other.

She looked away unhappily. 'I'm only having lunch with him.'

'Make sure that's all.'

Her cheeks flaming, she nearly choked on her coffee. 'That's a horrible thing to say . . .'

His mouth twisted wryly, as something in his eyes drew hers back to him again. His glance held a faint apology—she couldn't believe the plea for understanding. It made him seem vulnerable which she was sure he was not.

'Take no notice of me.' He shrugged. 'I must sound like a jealous husband, which I've no intention of even pretending to be, having just escaped Pearl.'

'Richard . . .' she gulped, but he didn't allow her to go on.

Getting to his feet, he said coolly, 'Instead of sitting

here talking nonsense, we'd be better employed getting to the office. I'm sure you're well able to look after yourself.'

Despite Richard's derisory remarks, she still looked forward to her lunch with Harry. She could relax with him completely. With him, there was none of the electric tension that could flare up so nerve-rackingly between Richard and herself.

'I wanted to know how Richard is,' she said, almost as soon as Harry picked her up. She was quite unconscious of the urgency in her voice and eyes, revealing that which she had hoped would remain a secret.

Harry sighed and made her wait until they reached the restaurant and ordered their meal. When he looked at her compassionately, it suddenly dawned on her that he had been giving her a few minutes to compose herself.

'You want to know how he is?' he repeated. 'I guess, otherwise, you wouldn't have agreed to come out with me?'

She flushed. 'Yes I would, though perhaps,' she confessed, 'not today. I haven't much time when I'm working, but you know how much I like you, Harry.'

'Am I supposed to gain comfort from that?' he jeered drily, then laughed. 'All right, love. I know when I'm beaten. Though what my cousin's got that I haven't, I just can't think!'

She didn't reply, not even when she knew he was half-joking—it would have brought too many things out into the open. Even a smile failed.

Harry patted her hand gently. 'At least Pearl has gone,' he said softly.

'Has she?' She glanced at him doubtfully, then took a grip on herself. Harry was kind but she must resist the temptation to weep on his shoulder. Pearl wasn't her business, anyway.

'It's Richard,' she said quickly, before Harry could comment. 'As usual, he won't tell me anything. I realise,' she went on, 'that you can't discuss your patients with all and sundry, but last night he looked so tired, I couldn't help feeling worried.'

'He still needs to take it easy,' Harry grimaced. 'I advised him to spend more time at home but I don't think his general health is a cause for worry. His eyes may improve. On the other hand, they may be as good as they'll ever be if he persists in using them nearly twenty-four hours a day. I hope, as far as that goes, that he is carrying out my instructions?'

'Wearing spectacles?'

'Yes.'

Christine's eyes were inexplicably damp. 'I haven't seen him wearing them myself, but I asked Miss Wright—his secretary, you know—this morning, and she swears that he is.'

'If I looked as distinguished as he does in them, I'd wear them whether I needed them or not.' Harry grinned ruefully. 'Women aren't the only ones who wish they'd been born with pretty faces.'

Christine laughed with him, knowing he was handsome enough to have nothing to worry about. She appreciated that he was trying to make her feel better but her laughter faded when he asked eventually, 'How did Richard manage to persuade you to leave Scotland?'

'He didn't persuade, he threatened,' she admitted wryly. 'Both Miss Wright's assistants were ill, well, one's having a baby, and he said I would be useful. I think,' she hesitated, 'he didn't like the idea of my being at Cragend by myself. It would have bothered him, apparently.

Harry looked thoughtful but he didn't ask anything more for a few moments, before enquiring casually, 'When did he tell you about Pearl?'

'You'll scarcely believe this,' she exclaimed without thinking. 'Not until we'd almost reached London when, apparently, their engagement had been off since Christmas.'

Harry made no comment on that either. Instead, he said, 'And you're living with him.'

'Staying with him,' she corrected, her face pink at the possible implication.

'That's what I meant.' Harry smiled innocently.

'Not for long though,' she stressed coldly, just in case he was getting the wrong idea. 'I'm moving out next week.'

'You are?' Harry's brows suddenly shot up like Richard's had a habit of doing. 'Where to?'

'My own small flat.'

Harry looked impressed and slightly puzzled, 'Whereabouts?'

She saw no reason not to tell him but felt dismayed at the direction the conversation was taking. She had wanted to see Harry to ask him a few things about Richard. Now it seemed that it was Harry who was asking questions about herself. She hadn't intended revealing half the things Harry was getting out of her with such remarkable ease.

'Markam Place,' she said shortly.

'Doesn't Richard own a block of flats around there?' he asked slowly.

'It's one of his,' she confessed.

Wondering what was coming next, Christine glanced at him warily but, surprisingly, his face cleared and he only said lightly, 'At least he's looking after you. Considering all you did for him, it's the least he could do. As soon as you get settled. I'll be around for a drink one evening.'

She enjoyed her lunch but got back to the office fifteen minutes late as Harry refused to hurry. Just as she left him he invited her to dinner the following evening.

'If Richard won't come, I'll pick you up myself, but I don't see why he shouldn't. There'll only be about ten of us but I'll give him a ring later.'

Miss Wright hadn't returned from her lunch. Christine felt relieved that she had the office to herself as there were several things she wanted to mull over. She was just sitting down at her desk, however, when Richard's door snapped open and she found him glaring at her.

'You're late.'

'Not very.' She made the mistake of trying to minimise her own crime.

'In future,' he grated, 'don't be so generous with my time.'

Trying to remember that he was quite within his rights to complain, she murmured, 'I'm sorry.'

Instead of placating him, her apology only appeared to incense. 'Couldn't tear yourself away, I suppose? The conversation, or something, must have been riveting.'

Christine clenched her hands at the sarcasm in his voice. 'Harry wants us both to go to dinner, tomorrow night,' she said quickly, hoping that this would please him.

It didn't. Harry was wished to some unmentionable place where, judging from the blackness of Richard's face, he would enjoy watching him burning.

'I can go on my own,' Christine breathed, getting really alarmed.

Her further attempts to appease was met by another hail of fury. 'Over my dead body!' he exclaimed. 'I'll take you if it kills me.'

'I'm sure Harry meant no harm,' she gulped.

'You ask me to believe that,' he snapped, 'when he gets you back late with your lipstick all gone.'

'That was the meal.' She flushed, wondering what he was getting at. 'Oh!' she exclaimed, as it suddenly dawned. 'What a horrible mind you have. Harry never even touched me.'

'Didn't he?' Suddenly she was jerked closer to him and he was shaking her. Then, as he must have realised what he was doing, he just as suddenly almost flung her from him. 'I'm sorry, Christine,' he said curtly. 'Just get out of my sight, will you.'

Scrubbing a cowardly tear from her cheek, she

stumbled into the cloakroom as it seemed the only place to retreat to. When she came out, after removing her coat, he was back in his office and Miss Wright had returned.

He sent her home at five in a taxi but it was Mrs Webster who told her that he wouldn't be in for dinner. Christine had hers on a tray in the lounge, blindly staring at a TV programme. She didn't flatter herself that Richard hadn't come home because she was there but she knew she had made him angry and she wished that he had given her a chance to make amends. He had apologised for shaking her but she didn't believe he had meant it. She had felt violence, not remorse in the hands which had gripped her, and she wondered for the thousandth time what she had done to cause it. If only he had come home and been frank with her, then she might have been able to put things right. She found it impossible to believe that her innocent lunch with Harry had been the cause of it; she was convinced it must be something else.

She lay awake, worrying, long after going to bed. It must have been two in the morning when she heard him come in. Consequently, she was late getting to sleep and overslept. Knowing that this could be another black mark against her, she showered and dressed in little more than five minutes and rushed down to the dining-room without bothering to see if she looked all right.

Richard had finished his breakfast—at least, he appeared to have had a cup of coffee. He was so grey that she stared at him in consternation, appalled that he looked almost ill again.

'You should have come home before you did,' she exclaimed, forgetting to be tactful. 'You look terrible.'

'How do you know what time I got in?' he asked sharply, ignoring her comment on his looks.

Christine bent her head over the toast she didn't want so that he wouldn't notice her pink cheeks. 'I . . . er, the noise you made woke me up.'

'Odd,' he mused, 'I don't remember making any noise.'

Didn't he consider that she might have been worried? Harry might maintain that he was fully recovered but the doubts and anxieties she had experienced over him in Scotland weren't easily disposed of. There were lines on his face and a hardness to his mouth that she was sure hadn't been there at Cragend, which seemed to indicate that in some way he was still suffering. And he had obviously been reading the morning paper without his spectacles!

Fastening on this, rather than begin on all the other things when there was so little time, she asked accusingly, 'Why aren't you wearing your glasses? Harry said you ought to.'

He glared at her balefully. 'Been discussing me, have you? I knew what the lunch was all about.'

Because she couldn't deny it, she countered unwisely, 'According to you, it was about worse things than that!'

'As well, then.' He continued glaring.

Suddenly she was weary. They couldn't take up where they'd left off yesterday! 'I realise that you feel responsible for me, Richard, which is why you worry when I go out with other men. Believe me, Harry may fool around but he treats me like a sister.' Almost, she thought.

Richard grunted. 'According to you, all men do.'

There was still antagonism in his voice but he did sound faintly mollified. Pressing what could be a fleeting advantage, she said quickly. 'I'll admit to asking Harry if you were really well again. Whether it's the truth or not, he said you were. He also said you must take care.'

'Christine!' The green eyes hardened again at her last remark. 'I refused to be hectored over something which, as I've told you before, is none of your business. I may look a weak specimen but I assure you I'm not.'

'P—people often feel weak but won't admit it,' she stammered unhappily.

'So.' He smiled deviously. 'In view of the fact that you think I need it for my health's sake, you'd advise an early night?'

'I certainly would,' she said fervently.

'Then before we leave, you had better ring Harry and inform him that we won't be coming tonight.'

'Oh . . .!' Her eyes widened in confusion. 'I forgot . . .'

'Never mind,' he jeered. 'He's very understanding.'

Her face paled. 'I can go myself. We can't both let him down.'

'Christine!' He sighed, throwing up his hands, though he did look slightly remorseful. 'Can't you see I'm not serious? You goad me into saying things I don't mean. I've spoken to Harry and everything's arranged. I'm taking you.' Pausing briefly, he asked, 'Do you have a suitable dress?'

'Yes.'

His brow quirked at her mutinous tone but she wasn't prepared to forgive him yet. 'Fine,' he said briefly; then, 'I have a phone call to make. If you go ahead and wait in the car, I'll join you in a minute.'

The day dragged, though Miss Wright kept Christine busy and was inclined to be chatty.

'Wendy's coming back on Monday,' she said, 'which should lighten your load. The firm's after a big contract in the Middle East. According to the night-watchmen, Richard was working on it until the early hours of the morning.'

So that was where he had been—and why he looked so tired. Christine flushed when she thought of where her suspicions had taken her.

'Will he get it?'

'He stands a good chance.' Miss Wright tapped her fingertips on her desk thoughtfully. 'Richard's a genius, when it comes to having the edge on his rivals. If he gets this, though, we could be saying goodbye to him for a while.'

A tremor ran down Christine's spine and she felt herself grow cold. Conscious of Miss Wright glancing at her expectantly, she made a project of fiddling with her typewriter. Keeping her eyes lowered and her voice light, she asked, 'Do you ever go with him?'

Miss Wright smiled wryly. 'Usually he takes a PA and hires local staff. Sometimes, if everything goes well, he leaves his PA to get on with it and doesn't stay long. I generally hold the fort here. I must confess that I'm getting too old to uproot and he knows it.'

So, it might not be long before Richard was gone from her life altogether. If he went abroad, she knew she wouldn't be here when he returned. As soon as she could, she must make plans of her own. Christine sighed and stuck another sheet of paper in her typewriter. She meant nothing to him, apart from someone to help. She had been foolish to think he might come to think of her as someone special.

On the way home that evening, she began to wish that she hadn't been going to Harry's dinner party. She wondered if it was sensible to go anywhere with Richard, or to accept any more help from him of any kind when she knew that she must make a complete break. Even the flat could be a mistake. He didn't have Pearl anymore but undoubtedly there would be other women, forever calling at the house or office and ringing him up. To have to witness his growing friendship with someone new might be more than she could bear.

Richard said that they would be leaving for Harry's at seven-thirty and before she got ready, Christine went to have a word with Mrs Webster. The housekeeper had caught a cold and she wanted to see how she was.

After Mrs Webster had assured her she was none the worse and that there was nothing she could do for her, Christine went upstairs. She had a blue dress, in a fine, silky velvet which the sales lady at the shop where she had brought it, had said exactly matched her eyes and looked lovely with her dark hair. She got it out of the wardrobe and laid it carefully on the bed before going to have a bath. She hoped she wasn't going to be overdressed but Harry had said that it was a dinner party and Richard had asked if she had anything suitable to wear. From both remarks she had concluded that something informal wouldn't do. She hoped she was right.

The bath water was hot and soothing and she left it reluctantly, wishing she could have soaked longer but it was already after seven and she had no desire to keep Richard waiting.

As she dried herself, she wondered what he would be wearing. A dark jacket and tie could be taken for granted but she felt a sharp thrill run through her as she tried to imagine what he would look like all dressed up. She had only seen him in casual clothes and dark suits so far but she guessed that his tall, powerful figure would look good in almost anything.

After dusting herself liberally with talcum powder, she slipped into new satin undies and made up her face. Her new make-up went on like a dream. A little eye-shadow and mascara made her eyes seem huge and their colour deeper, while the subtle pink gloss she used on her mouth emphasised the soft fullness of her lips. Even her hair behaved beautifully. The hairdresser had cut it cleverly, making the most of its natural thickness and colour. It curled attractively over her small head, a perfect foil for her long, slender neck and delicate features.

With two minutes to spare, she flung a coat over her arm and ran downstairs. Richard, pacing the hall, spun on his heel as he heard her coming. His eyes fixed on the picture she made in her long blue velvet dress and she thought she saw him go pale.

'Richard?' She was frightened that he was ill again. 'Are you all right?'

'Of course.' Some of the tension eased out of him, as if he deliberately forced himself to relax. His glance moved over her slowly, pausing on her high, taut breasts, just visible beneath the low cut bodice. He smiled grimly. 'I think you stopped my breath for a second. Did you do it on purpose?'

She laughed, thinking he was teasing her. 'It must be my dress. The woman I bought it from said it would be a success.'

He pretended to frown severely. 'Is that what she calls depriving men of their breath?'

'Richard . . .' Christine's voice was suddenly unsteady as their eyes became locked and their faces inexplicably sobered. 'Richard . . .' she whispered again, swaying towards him, feeling like a stem bent by the wind.

His arms were reaching out to gather her to him, when he paused abruptly and took hold of her coat instead.

'It's cold out, you'll need this,' he said, as their taxi-driver rang the bell. 'It should have been a fur.'

She shook her head numbly as he buttoned it for her. 'I'll be warm enough.'

Richard preferred to use taxis when he went out in the evenings. Everywhere they went it was either by taxi or car. As she settled down beside him, Christine stared dully through the window and thought of the walks they had taken in Scotland. She didn't miss Cragend nearly as much as she missed the sense of companionship Richard and she had shared there. Their relationship may have been stormy at times but they had shared a certain closeness that made her heart ache with a sense of frustration whenever she thought of it.

Richard looked as striking as she had known he would in evening dress. He may have thought she hadn't noticed, but she had. His jacket was velvet which, somehow, lent a hint of sensuality to the hard line of his mouth. At Harry's, she observed the immediate attention he received from the female guests and she was aware of a wild surge of jealousy which she knew she must curb if she wasn't to have a very painful evening.

Harry's apartment was huge and superbly modern, the staff discreet. Surprisingly they were the first there and Richard drew her into the lounge, leaving Harry to welcome his other guests.

'How does he afford it?' Christine murmured, rather awe-struck by the sheer luxury of it all.

'His parents left him a pile.' Richard seemed singularly unimpressed, though he admitted, 'he hasn't done so badly himself.'

That must be an understatement. She watched as the large, thickly carpeted lounge gradually filled up. Trays of drinks were brought around. Richard helped himself to whisky and passed her a glass of something that seemed to be mostly orange juice. She didn't mind orange juice, in fact she usually preferred it, but she did mind being treated like a teenager and a very young teenager at that.

There were ten other guests besides themselves, she eventually counted. They were mostly doctors, both men and women. Among those who weren't, there was one man who glanced at her curiously.

'Aren't you Keith Colwell's daughter?' he startled Christine by asking, catching her alone for a few minutes when someone detained Richard.

When she nodded, he exclaimed, 'I thought I recognised you. You obviously don't remember me but your father used to work for my father's firm. We were sorry to hear of his death.'

CHAPTER NINE

CHRISTINE paled as she stared at the man who had reminded her of the past so abruptly. He must be in his early thirties and very presentable but she had no recollection of him.

'I'm sorry,' she said stiltedly. 'I'm afraid I didn't catch your name when Harry introduced us. I thought it was Brown but I couldn't be sure. If I had, I probably wouldn't have connected you with my father's old firm, anyway. You must be Cyril Brown's son?'

'Neil,' he supplied with a smile. 'And you only met me once so I'll forgive you for forgetting. I called at your house, one evening, for a quick word with your Dad. You were home from school, I believe.'

Christine still didn't remember but felt warmed that he did. 'I must have let you in?'

'You did,' he replied, then his expression changed. 'Your father was a great loss to the firm. Dad was sorry when he went but he couldn't persuade him to stay. He was upset when he heard of his death.' Neil's eyes quickened with interest over her lovely face. 'You will have to let me take you to see him, one day. I know he would be pleased.'

'I'd like that,' she agreed, not sure that she would but not liking to refuse. She smiled at Neil warmly, to make up for a lack of enthusiasm.

Out of the corner of her eye, she caught Richard glancing at her narrowly. He was standing a few yards away talking to a blonde and, as she remembered that Pearl was a blonde, she found herself wondering if he liked fair women best. She heard Neil asking if he could give her a ring that weekend and she nodded vaguely.

The blonde, she saw, laid a hand on Richard's arm as if to reclaim his wandering attention. He withdrew his hard eyes from Christine's face and smiled at her lazily.

At dinner, to Christine's surprise, Harry sat her beside him. 'It's the only chance I'm going to get to speak to you,' he teased. 'You appear to be enjoying instant success. How many men have asked to take you out?'

Two—but she wasn't about to tell Harry that as she had no intention of going out with either of them, unless, perhaps, with Neil Brown to see his father. One day she might date other men, once she got over Richard, but at the moment he filled her heart and thoughts to the exclusion of everyone else.

After dinner, someone switched on the stereo and couples began dancing. Christine hoped that Richard would ask her to dance with him as it could be the last chance she would get to be in his arms. She was disappointed—though she tried to hide it—when he ignored her and continued talking to the young blonde doctor who had remained glued to his side all evening. Other men invited Christine to dance and she was soon in demand as she was good to look at and light on her feet, but it gave her little pleasure. When Neil Brown held her close and whispered flirtatiously in her ear, it was for another man's arms that she yearned.

Some time after midnight, when Richard suggested it was time to leave, she agreed readily. Harry made no attempt to persuade them to stay longer and she was grateful. She felt tired and Neil's attentions had been getting a little too much for her. She was glad to go home.

'I'll be in touch next week.' Harry kissed her fondly. 'I may be able to help when you move into your new flat, unless you already have a string of young men queuing up for the privilege.'

All the way home, Richard was strangely silent, so much so that Christine was puzzled. Hadn't she complied with his wishes that evening? He had told her to socialise and she had. She was sure that she hadn't made an exhibition of herself, neither had she clung to his side and refused to mix.

As he locked the front door behind them, she said a quick good night, believing it wiser not to linger, when he so clearly had nothing more to say to her. In that, however, she discovered she was mistaken.

'Not so fast,' he snapped, as she turned towards the stairs. 'I'd like a word with you.'

His hand closing swiftly on her wrist made it impossible for her to escape, even had she wanted to, as he dragged her into the lounge. She gazed at him indignantly when he released her, as her wrist was sore from the pressure he exerted.

'There was no need to use force,' she said quietly.

'You couldn't wait to get away from me.'

She frowned. Did he realise how often he used that phrase? 'I thought you wanted to be alone,' she retorted. 'You hardly spoke to me on the way home.'

'I thought you would be tired after all the flirting you'd done,' he replied sarcastically. 'I don't know why I worried about you. You are certainly no Cinderella!'

'I never pretended to be,' she snapped back. 'And I was talking, not flirting. Harry's guests were very easy to talk to.'

Richard's lips curled as he considered her silently for a few seconds. 'I thought I should warn you about Neil Brown,' he said coldly. 'He has quite a reputation.'

'I'd be surprised if he hadn't, at his age,' she retorted in much the same tone. 'You have, yourself, but that's not to say it's based wholly on fact.'

'Really?' he murmured silkily. 'And what do you know of my reputation?'

'Not very much,' she admitted with a flush, 'but you must have known plenty of women . . .'

'I have known plenty of women,' he grated. 'But I like to believe I never took advantage of the innocent.'

'What a nasty thing to say! Harry didn't . . .'

'Some circumstances call for strong language.'

Perhaps, but she had done nothing tonight to justify

it. Her blue eyes flashed. 'You may believe what you say is warrantable but I do not! Apart from that, how many times do I have to tell you that I'm quite old enough to be able to think for myself, to accept total responsibility for everything I do . . .'

'Are you?' he interjected harshly, his face suddenly savage as he advanced and took hold of her. 'You chose to laugh at what you obviously consider out-dated concern. It might be more practical to demonstrate to you some of the dangers that indiscriminate behaviour can invite.'

'Oh, please . . .!' Feeling that everything was getting out of hand, Christine gazed at him appealingly, her eyes wide.

His were dark and glittering, his face washed of all warmth. Suddenly they were no longer employer and employee, self-appointed guardian and ward or whatever. They were simply man and woman. Christine felt the shift in their relationship so perceptibly that her breath caught sharply in her throat.

The man holding her took the strangled sound for fear and muttered tersely, 'It's too late for second thoughts.'

'Richard.' She tried to reason with him, not wanting him to do anything he might regret, but her pleading words were lost against his marauding lips.

His arms slid right around her and tightened as his mouth found hers, he paused only briefly as she tensed like a small, wild animal in a trap. Then her eyes half-closed as she felt a familiar molten sensation stir inside her, exactly as she remembered it from that night in her bedroom at Cragend. This startled her by being even more acute, as if the residue from that other time and emotion had been fermenting and was now about to explode.

Lifting his head, he was immediately aware of the physical response she would have liked to deny but couldn't. Her breath caught again at the burning look in his eyes, a naked hunger both frightening and incredibly exciting. This, too, she had known before, and only with him. She felt hot with a feverish weakness spreading right through her body. Giving in to it, she sagged against him revealingly.

He didn't speak. She realised that, unusually for him, he had consumed a lot of whisky at Harry's. Dazedly she wondered whether this could be responsible for his uncharacteristic behaviour, but she could have sworn that on the way home, he was completely sober. The glitter in his eyes must be the triumph he derived at her utter inability to escape him.

Didn't he realise that whatever he was trying to prove to her, none of it was necessary. She loved him, which made it impossible for her to respond to other men. As if attempting to convince him of this, she put her arms around his neck and met his descending mouth fervently, kissing him back with all the pent-up emotion she had had sealed up inside her for far too long.

Again, he mistook her response. 'Not so innocent, after all, are we?' she heard him mutter against her trembling lips. 'I was curious at Cragend but no one could kiss like that without previous experience.'

'You're mistaken,' she whispered.

'Am I?' he mocked.

His confidence in his own judgment shook her, jerking her from the cloud of rapture she'd been floating on, back to harsh reality. As her defence mechanism re-asserted itself, she tried to wedge a barrier between them with her hands, but this only served, as she encountered his hair roughened chest, to defeat her purpose by stimulating her senses like an electric current running through her nervous system. Sometime, while he was kissing her, she must have unbuttoned his shirt without realising what she was doing.

She felt Richard's breath fanning her face, then his mouth exploring hers more forcibly. The hand, which had rested lightly on her back, now pressed against her spine bringing her much more closely to him. She was completely caught up in the powerful spell of his dark sensuality which she hadn't been entirely conscious of until this moment. Becoming rapidly absorbed by it, the shock of her own physical awareness was overwhelming, as it turned her swiftly into a being she scarcely recognised.

Richard's kisses were soul-shaking, his urgent caresses devastating. All inclination to evade him faded as she became lost to the insiduous demands of a terrible hunger. Again her arms wound about his neck and she could do nothing to stop them.

He was holding her so tightly she could feel his heart pounding against her own like a sledge-hammer. The pressure of his arms hurt, his mouth was so violent she thought she might suffocate. She tasted blood on her tongue but, despite this she knew that she was welcoming the cruelty of his assault, not rejecting it.

Then, as suddenly as he had swooped, he lifted his head and stared savagely down at her. 'I want you,' he muttered harshly.

She was appalled by the raw violence in his voice and dismayed to find herself responding to it in exactly the same way. Something was happening to her. Staring at him, she eventually focused properly, and what she saw in his eyes made her own heart race correspondingly. She felt that she was being taken over by emotions and needs completely new to her, which she only vaguely understood but could no longer dismiss.

When he lifted her and carried her upstairs, she couldn't manage a word of protest. She could only cling to him, letting the consuming force of his passion flow over and through her.

Closing her bedroom door with the heel of his shoe, he laid her on the bed. He didn't flick on the light but if he had she may not have noticed. The blazing desire inside her made her unconscious of any darkness.

She heard him groan as he went on kissing her and her mouth moved convulsively under his. 'Put your arms around me,' he muttered against her lips and she obeyed his ragged command. He had thrown off his jacket and her hands found the heavy muscles of his shoulders under his shirt. She had been as close to him before but with nothing like the same volume of feeling between them. For the first time she felt they were sharing the same thoughts and desires.

He dealt impatiently with her dress, removing it, along with his own clothes, in a series of economical movements. His mouth burned as he trailed it down her neck to the racing pulse in her throat, scorching her skin until it felt on fire. Breathless sounds escaped her, while he muttered repeatedly, 'I want you.'

His arms were around her, holding her tightly, then they slackened to allow him to explore her eager young body. Her bra proved no barrier to his seaching hands, in seconds he had found the fastener and discarded it. She swallowed as he kissed her naked breasts and fondled them. When he took her nipples between his finger and thumb and bit gently, she thought she would die from the volume of feeling shooting through her.

No one had ever touched her so intimately and even Richard, until now, had never touched her with such a degree of passion. She could feel the aroused heat of his thighs against hers, demanding her response, full of an urgency that needed no explanation.

'Richard,' she murmured huskily, overflowing with desire herself, her one wish to give herself to him, but having no idea how to make this any clearer to him than she was doing. Yet when she tried to speak more than his name, some innate part of her shrank from committing herself by words to absolute surrender.

Yet she couldn't prevent herself from drowning in the aching pleasure of his love making. As he caressed her, she caressed him back, her courage increasing, growing bolder. Her palms tingled from the roughness of the hair on his chest and she let them drift over the leanness of his hips to his powerful thighs. She was dimly aware of the faint musky smell of him filling her lungs from the warmth of his skin as his lips returned to hers again.

This time his kisses were deeper and harder yet softened sensually as he began arching over her, letting their bodies come close then impinging himself on her in a way that inflamed her senses to a height that was almost unbearable. The blood throbbed through her veins, she lost all count of time, she could only hear her ears ringing from the way her heart was pounding. She whispered Richard's name as the world whirled away, leaving just the two of them, lost in a red hot void of spinning space.

The skin on Richard's back was wet and he was gasping, as if he was physically suffering. The hardness of his body increased but just as she thought he was about to take her, he went completely still and raised a rigid hand to her cheek.

'You're crying!' he exclaimed.

'No . . .' she breathed.

'Christine!' he snapped, releasing her.

It was like the breath of a cold wind. His body stiffened against her clinging hands as he moved away. She felt the chill of some dreadful premonition turning all the lovely warmth between them to ice.

'Don't go,' she begged, trying to explain. There were tears on her cheeks but only because of the force of her emotions. 'I'm not really crying,' she said helplessly. 'I wasn't frightened . . .'

'I am,' he retorted bluntly, keeping his face averted. 'I told you, I don't prey on innocent young women. You should thank God for your tears, whatever the reason for them. They made me realise exactly what I was doing.'

'Innocence has nothing to do with it,' she stressed desperately, knowing that if he went now, he would never come back. 'A girl usually only keeps her innocence, as you call it, for the man she will eventually love.'

'Exactly what I'm trying to tell you,' he rapped, misunderstanding what she was trying to tell him. 'It's unusual, today, for a girl to remain chaste. If you've managed to, so far, how could I possibly destroy what you are keeping for another man. You would hate me.'

'No,' she groaned, 'You've got it all wrong. I love you, Richard,' she made herself look at him steadily, though it wasn't easy. 'That's why I want to belong to you, no matter what happens afterwards . . .'

She might have shot him. Even in the darkness, his face seemed to take on a paler hue. 'You're letting gratitude exaggerate your true feelings, Christine. That, and the proximity we shared at Cragend. If I did consider that you owed me anything, I wouldn't want that kind of repayment. As for loving me, I doubt if you really know what love is.'

He talked quickly and savagely. She couldn't get a word in until he had finished. 'I do know what love is,' she contradicted. 'There's no truth in anything you've just said . . .'

'Just shut up, will you, Christine,' he interrupted. Rising abruptly from the edge of the bed where he'd been sitting, he stared down on her cringing form. 'Let's put it this way, we both got a little carried away but nothing's happened that can't be forgotten. I, regretfully, was over-protective, believing you weren't able to look after yourself, and drinking too much whisky didn't help. I ought to be old enough at my age,' he added enigmatically, 'to realise I can't drown my sorrows, but apparently I'm not infallible.'

Pearl! The other woman's name slammed into Christine's head with the heat of a branding iron. How could she have forgotten Pearl? It was Pearl whom he loved, he had as good as admitted she had broken his heart.

As he bent to pick up his shirt after pulling on his trousers, she managed an admirable giggle which she hoped might save her pride. 'You're quite right, Richard,' she said ruefully. 'I'll admit that I didn't realise what I was inviting—if you drank too much at Harry's party then so did I. Neil would insist . . .' She let her voice trail off as if she was reminiscing privately and with amusement, while she was really drawing another excruciating breath. 'I'm sorry if I embarrassed you, Richard. I do love you in a way. You've been very kind to me but, as you say . . .'

'Good night, Christine.' His taut voice cut her off decisively and was so full of contempt that even before her door slammed, she realised that she had achieved her objective. But at what cost? Burying her face in a pillow, Christine wept fresh tears, tears which Richard would have been right in thinking were of real unhappiness.

The next morning when she got down he was gone. Mrs Webster told her he'd had an urgent phone call and had left for the office straight afterwards.

'Did he look all right?' Christine wasn't sure why she asked and when she noticed Mrs Webster giving her a sharp glance, she said quickly. 'I thought he seemed tired, last night.'

Mrs Webster frowned. 'I can't say I noticed that much but he certainly sounded all right. Must be something big going on because he wouldn't stop for breakfast.'

When Christine reached the office, Miss Wright said that he had gone overseas but expected to be back on Sunday evening.

'Mrs Webster said he'd had an urgent call.' Christine managed a smile with an effort. 'Is it the Middle East?'

'No,' Miss Wright revealed vaguely. 'It's another contract we're after. Our plans and quotations are already in and some officials want to see him.'

'It sounds promising.'

Miss Wright shrugged. 'It may be, but like all contracts, you can't be absolutely sure until you've got it.'

Christine removed the cover from her typewriter, wondering why she should feel so depressed. Richard was away, she wouldn't have to endure his stony glances, and his absence would give her time to put the fiasco of the previous evening behind her.

Miss Wright said that Richard had asked her to ring Mrs Webster and let her know that he wouldn't be home for a few days and she asked Christine to do it. When Christine spoke to her, she asked her not to make a large dinner on her account, and said that she would just as soon have an omelette or something light on a tray. She even felt guilty over that, as she didn't dare suggest she could cook it herself and guessed that the only time Mrs Webster took a break from cooking was when Richard was out or away.

The day crawled by, though she was busy enough, as Miss Wright was seldom off the phone and she had to cope with a lot of things with which she wasn't familiar.

'It's what's called being thrown in at the deep end,' Miss Wright said sympathetically. 'It's at times like this that I can particularly use someone with intelligence.'

Christine was warmed by the other woman's praise, which she wasn't sure she deserved. Throughout the day, she had found herself too often forgetting everything but the memory of Richard's kisses. He had blamed what had happened on having too much to drink, and while she realised this might have been partly true, she suspected he had got carried away by pretending it was Pearl he held in his arms, rather than just a girl who worked for him.

Christine knew she would treasure the hour they had shared all her life. She would forget she had been used as a substitute and remember only the bliss of it. She could be a fool, she undoubtedly was, but at least to live briefly in a fool's paradise might be better than never having lived at all? She refused to consider what might have happened if Richard hadn't slammed on the brakes. He had, so it was no use conjecturing, but if the outcome had been different she didn't think she would have regretted anything.

On Saturday, rather than sit moping all day, she agreed to go with Neil Brown to meet his father. When she arrived she was, in fact, invited for lunch and made much of. Both of Neil's parents were very nice to her.

His father said that there was always a place in his organisation for bright young people, despite the present difficulties, while his mother was soon confiding that Neil's unmarried state worried them and that they would like grandchildren. Christine supposed she should feel flattered that they welcomed her so warmly into the family circle, but she knew she couldn't take advantage of their kindness by pretending that she was interested in Neil, other than as a friend.

She left after tea, refusing to stay for dinner or to spend the evening elsewhere with Neil. She was even reluctant to agree that he should give her a ring the following week.

Sunday she spent on her own, wandering about London, visiting places of which she had been particularly fond. Yet she discovered no great affinity with any of them. She was unable to find the sense of belonging for which she was looking. She felt like a lost spirit searching for a home. One day she must put down roots and map out a proper career for herself but, for the moment, she had no idea where to begin.

She knew an intense desire to be alone for a while, even for a few days, somewhere where she could think about her future properly. In Scotland she must have had plenty of opportunity but she hadn't been able to see clearly. Now that she thought she could, she was bogged down by so many things that there might not be a chance.

Having promised Mrs Webster that she would be home before dark, she tried to be, so that she wouldn't worry her. It was just after six when she let herself in and she was surprised to find the housekeeper waiting for her, looking decidedly put out.

'What's wrong?' Christine's quick smile faded. 'I didn't think I was that late.'

'You aren't,' Mrs Webster hissed. 'It's her, not you that's wrong.' She nodded towards the lounge.

'Her?'

'Mrs Kristol!' Mrs Webster exclaimed disgustedly. 'She's been here for the past hour.'

Christine tried not to look as shocked as she felt. 'Did she come with Richard?'

'No, he isn't back yet,' Mrs Webster said sullenly. 'I've told Mrs Kristol I've no idea when he will be, either, but she insists on waiting. I don't know what to do, or what he'll say. Could you go and speak to her?'

'Oh, Mrs Webster.' Christine bit her lip, 'Must I? She and I didn't exactly hit it off in Scotland. She doesn't like me and even if she would take any notice of me, I can't really ask her to leave . . .'

'Well . . . we can't leave her sitting there on her own, can we? I mean,' Mrs Webster sighed, 'what would Mr Richard say?'

'All right.' Christine squared her slender shoulders, though her heart felt like lead. 'I'll go and say hello though I won't promise much more. I doubt if she will appreciate even that from me.'

Mrs Webster retreated to her kitchen and Christine frowned uneasily as she slipped out of the jacket she was wearing over her jeans. She took her time opening the lounge door. Pearl wasn't going to like her being here, and though she tried to tell herself that it was none of Pearl's business, it did nothing to bolster her courage.

Pearl, who was sitting on a sofa with her shoes off and her legs curled under her, managed to look far more elegant and attractive than plenty of people did sitting normally. When she saw Christine, however, her casual poise underwent a distinct change.

'I thought I heard Richard!' she exclaimed. 'What the hell are you doing here?'

Sometimes Christine wondered herself. 'I'm only staying for a few days until I move into my own accommodation,' she replied coldly. 'Richard is away.'

'So that fool of a housekeeper keeps telling me,' Pearl snapped. 'She's been repeating it every five minutes since I arrived but I'm not leaving until I see him.'

If there was any hope of getting rid of Pearl, it would take tact. To avoid what she suspected could easily become a very difficult situation, Christine kept control of her own temper. 'We have no definite idea when he will be home, Pearl. It could be this evening but just as likely tomorrow, or another week. You've been in the business, or rather your late husband was. You must know what it's like.'

'I certainly had no idea what went on behind the scenes,' Pearl sneered tartly, referring, Christine was startled to realise, to herself. 'Quite a little schemer, aren't you? I knew I wasn't wrong about you in Scotland.'

Christine later shuddered to think what more Pearl would have said if they hadn't been interrupted at that precise moment by a noise in the hall. As both women paused uncertainly, the lounge door, swung open as Richard strode through it. Christine felt slightly sick when he ignored her but seemed delighted to see his ex-fiancée.

'Why, Pearl,' he exclaimed, a smile warming his dark face. 'This is a pleasant surprise.'

'Oh, Richard!' Rushing to him, Pearl's voice actually trembled, though Christine caught the flash of triumph in her eyes. She watched incredulously as Pearl flung her arms around him and whimpered, 'I knew you would be pleased to see me. I was such a fool to leave you. I couldn't wait any longer to discover whether you would forgive me but I must have been a bigger fool to have had any doubts.'

'I've been abroad,' he murmured, his hands going to her shoulders.

'I know . . .!' Pearl sounded choked with remorse and tears. 'If only you'd told me, I could have come with you. As it is . . .'

Christine closed the door quietly behind her as Richard murmured something more. He still hadn't spoken to her, though she had felt him shoot her a quick glance as she went out. It was as she had known it would be if Pearl came back. Richard had welcomed her with open arms. Neither of them appeared to be sparing a thought for the man Pearl was supposed to have left him for. Christine wondered if he had ever existed.

Richard must love her deeply to have forgiven her so immediately—that must prove the depth of his love. Christine drew a shuddering breath, waiting until she stopped trembling, then she went and told a disapproving Mrs Webster that it looked as if Pearl would be staying for dinner and asked whether she would mind if she collected hers on a tray and had it in her room.

On Monday, when she arrived home from work alone, having seen nothing of Richard all day, she found a letter from Ken Granger awaiting her. Feeling a little ashamed for not getting in touch with him, she carried it to her room. She was curious to know how he had obtained her address.

Ken was indignant, as she had thought he might be, that she hadn't told him she was going. 'What a terrible way to treat an old friend,' he wrote.

> 'I had to seek out old Jamie and it was only coincidence that he had Mr Kingsley's address. He doesn't know if you are staying with him, though; that's why I put please forward on the envelope. Anyway, wherever you are, I hope you get this in time, for I'm being married on Saturday and I'd like you to be there. Pam, bless her red head, has agreed to marry me at last and I'm not giving her a chance to change her mind. If you don't have time to reply, it doesn't matter. Just come. My folks will put you up and there's a place reserved for you at the reception—so here's hoping.' Love, Ken.

Christine re-read the letter and then gazed at it for a long time. It would be nice to go to Ken's wedding, but out of the question. She would write after it was over and explain and send a present. It would be a big wedding as both sets of parents were well off. She smiled as she imagined what it would be like, the women gaily dressed, their men big and brawny in swinging kilts, the skirl of the pipes. With a sigh, she tore up the letter and slipped the enclosed invitation into her bag to keep as a memento, not as something she anticipated using.

After taking a quick shower and putting on a light dress, she joined Mrs Webster for dinner. Richard was dining out. He had informed them that he wouldn't be coming home until later, from which they had both assumed—though they didn't discuss it—that he would be dining with Pearl. Throughout breakfast he had kept his nose buried in the morning papers and when he had driven Christine to work, he'd had scarcely two words to say to her. Not that she'd had much to say herself. She had felt more dead than alive through not being able to sleep for thinking of him.

The following morning it was much the same. Richard was apparently determined to ignore her. She knew that he was seeing Pearl again but what hurt almost as much, was his apparent assumption that if he gave Christine the least encouragement she would make a nuisance of herself. Then Wendy Millar was restored to health and back at the office. And while this certainly lightened Christine's work load, as Miss Wright had said it would, it also, on occasion, made her feel almost surplus to requirements. Wendy was a nice girl and they had taken to each other immediately, but this didn't help much when there were long hours to fill and little else but tortured thoughts to fill them with.

That evening, Richard did come home but spent most of it in his study. He even ate there, something he had never chosen to do since leaving Scotland. This, Christine felt, was another rebuff, and while she knew she had to see him, she had to steel herself to approach him.

'Yes?' he barked, as she knocked on the study door. 'What is it?'

Refusing to speak through the door, she opened it and went in, though he didn't invite her to. Closing it behind her, she paused as she stared at him. He may have Pearl back and, according to Miss Wright, he had a lucrative contract tied up, but none of it seemed to be doing much for him. He looked haggard. Harry had been called to New York for a few weeks—he'd left a message with Mrs Webster on Saturday—otherwise she would have given him a ring and told him about it. Briefly she forgot about Pearl. If Richard wasn't careful he could have a relapse.

'Can't you see I'm busy?' he snapped, when she didn't say anything but just stood regarding him silently.

'Oh,' she flushed. 'Yes, I'm sorry. All I actually wanted was the key for the apartment. You said that it would be ready tomorrow.'

He frowned and laid down the pen he was using. Christine's eyes widened at the doodles that covered the pad in front of him. She wondered what he had on his mind but knew better than to ask.

'I was being optimistic,' he replied curtly. 'I'm afraid you'll have to wait longer.'

'How long?'

'Another week perhaps.' He shrugged, and, as her eyes darkened doubtfully, he rapped, 'You don't think I'm trying to keep you here deliberately, do you?'

'No.' She couldn't believe that—and it wouldn't have mattered about the flat if things had been different between them. Suddenly inspiration surged through her. What if she could find a place for herself? There was just a chance that Neil Brown might be able to help.

'It's okay.' She shrugged, achieving a smile which she hoped appeared cool. 'In fact, I may not need it.'

'Oh?' He took hold of the pen again and she noticed, because, despite everything, she was anxious about him, how white his knuckles were. 'What do you mean, you may not need it?' he asked.

'I may not need your job either,' she prevaricated, 'I've been—well, considering other things.'

The green eyes glinted piercingly as he raised his head. 'Please be more explicit.'

Who did he think he was, demanding, commanding, just as he had done at Cragend. 'I'm sorry but I can't be, not at the moment,' she improvised wearily. 'Any new plans I make may not just involve myself, but it's not something we need discuss. I would have liked to have moved out tomorrow, if only because you must want the house to yourself. Since Pearl has come back, it must be awkward for you, having one of your employees living here.'

'Christine!' His teeth snapped. 'Just what the hell are you getting at?'

'I—I know it's none of my business,' she stammered, her blue eyes anguished. 'I didn't mean to talk about that . . .'

'Well forget the rest,' he almost snarled. 'You don't know what you are talking about so let that suffice.'

'Richard?'

He threw up a silencing hand. 'I have work to do and I would appreciate it if you'd let me get on with it. And,' he added harshly, as she turned with drooping shoulders to obey, 'if you do make any fresh plans, perhaps you wouldn't mind letting me know about them, before you leave.'

CHAPTER TEN

SHE couldn't stay any longer. Christine decided the next day at work that she would have to get away. Richard's attitude the previous evening had hurt more than she would have thought possible but, in retrospect, she had realised that he wasn't entirely to blame. She had got up that morning intending somehow to make her peace with him, only to discover that he had gone. Not to the office but abroad again for another few days, to a place he hadn't disclosed. All Mrs Webster could tell her was that he hadn't said when he would be back. It was Miss Wright who told her that he wasn't away on business but whether she knew where he was or not, she didn't say and Christine didn't ask. It wasn't difficult to string a few relevant facts together and guess he was with Pearl.

While it was easy to decide that she couldn't stay in his house nor in his employment any longer, it wasn't until she left the office at five on the Friday following Richard's departure that she knew exactly what she was going to do.

Using the first phone she could find, she rang Euston and booked a night sleeper to Inverness. Her father had used the service quite often. She would go to Ken's wedding—he was being married the following day—then go on to stay at Cragend. And she would leave a note for Richard, telling him she had resigned.

Mrs Webster wasn't in when she got home. There was a note on the hall table informing Christine that she had gone to see her doctor and would make a light supper for them when she returned.

She was back by the time Christine had packed and dismissed her anxious enquiry. 'Just my cold.' She shrugged. 'Well, that's getting better but it seems to have left me deaf. I can't hear what people are saying sometimes and I thought I'd better see about it while Mr Richard is still away or he's going to get tired of having to shout at me.'

'What had your doctor to say?' Christine frowned.

'Nothing, really. He seems to think it will go away in its own time, if I have patience.'

Christine felt worried over leaving Mrs Webster on her own but she realised she might be a lot better for a few days rest with no one to look after. When she saw her looking curiously at her suitcase, she tried to explain that she was going to Scotland, as a friend was getting married.

'Getting married!' Mrs Webster's kindly eyes widened with startled surprise. 'Well, I never! Sudden, was it?'

'I think so.' Christine nodded.

'Well, I never,' Mrs Webster said again, rubbing what looked suspiciously like a tear from her eye. 'I hope you will both be very happy, dear. There's nothing like a nice wedding, I always says, for having a good cry. I would loved to have been there, if only to have thrown some confetti.'

Christine drew a sharp breath. Surely Mrs Webster didn't think . . .? No, it wasn't possible. She hadn't been paying much attention. She must have said that she hoped they would be very happy.

'Mrs Webster . . .' she began, thinking she should make sure, but just then the doorbell rang. 'Oh, damn! That must be my taxi,' she explained.

'You'd better hurry, dear. You don't want to miss your . . . How are you travelling?'

'Train!' Christine shouted.

'Plane?' Mrs Webster murmured, waving goodbye from the door, leaving Christine with the crazy conviction, now too late to confirm, that her former suspicions might be correct.

The train was half empty, which wasn't surprising on such a cold winter's night. Christine hoped that it wouldn't snow. Snow wasn't forecast but at this time of year, especially in the Highlands, the weather could change in a few hours. She made plans before she went to sleep, or rather, she went over and ratified those she had made earlier. In Inverness, she would hire a car and, after Ken was married, she would drive to Cragend. It wasn't that she was homesick for Cragend but she was certain that it was the only place where she would be able to think out her problems. And she wasn't exactly spoiled for choice, she thought bitterly. Even if nothing else came of the weekend, it would be nice to see old friends again.

When she returned to London, if she didn't have anything else sorted out, she would stay in a modest hotel until she found other accommodation. She could easily afford to, as she still had quite a bit of money left, despite spending some on clothes.

On the other hand, she might find work in Scotland, for the spring and summer. After a few days at Cragend, she was sure that she would have a much better idea of what she must do.

She didn't think she would sleep but the motion of the train eventually had a lulling effect and her eyelids closed. She knew nothing more until the sleeping-car attendant knocked on her door with a cup of tea.

Inverness was dark and unwelcoming at eight o'clock on a winter's morning. Rousing herself, Christine drank her hot tea and got dressed. It was no use feeling apprehensive at this stage, she told herself sternly.

Later, she went to the nearby hotel and had a steaming pot of coffee and forced down some bacon and eggs and toast. The meal was well cooked and delicious but she only ate it because she didn't know when her next one might be. Before she shopped for a wedding present, she set about hiring a car and discovering the whereabouts of the church where Ken was to be married.

At twelve, she returned to the church and by one-thirty she was at the reception wishing Ken and a radiant Pam the best of everything. She managed to whisper to Ken that she wouldn't be staying long at the reception because she was going on to Cragend. Ken couldn't very well argue, with dozens of guests still lined up, waiting their turn to congratulate him and kiss the bride, but he did manage to ask if she was crazy and advised her to think again.

She didn't take his advice but as she drove out of the city, she thought that it was nice of him to be concerned. She didn't think she would have stayed for the whole reception anyway. The ceremony had been about as much as she could take. She had begun thinking of Richard and she had thought that her heart might break.

The frost was still intense. It might be too cold for snow but the darkness of the sky looked threatening and the journey, not normally over-long, seemed to take ages.

While she was shopping for Ken's present, she had remembered to buy some supplies. There wouldn't be anything at Cragend but at least she knew that even if she was stormbound, she wouldn't run short of anything for a while. There would be enough fuel in the house, since Richard had ordered enough coke to last all winter.

Old Jamie almost dropped when he saw her but he parted with the house keys willingly enough.

'I've been there every day,' he informed her. 'It should be all right. Mind you,' he frowned, 'it's not the time of year for a slip of a girl like yourself to be there on her own. Does Mr Kingsley know?'

'I have lived there by myself before, Jamie,' she replied evasively.

'I never thought it right, though.'

'I'll only be staying for a night or two,' she hastened to assure him. 'I'll have the keys back to you by Monday at the latest.'

'I'll look by,' Jamie promised, 'to see if you need anything.'

Christine didn't linger after enquiring after his health.

Cragend loomed in front of her out of the gathering darkness in a very few minutes. Parking the car haphazardly in front of it, she let herself in.

Strangely, as she closed the door behind her, she felt nothing. There was no sense of homecoming, no feeling of being unwelcome, either. The past months might never have been. Incredibly she felt that this was just another day, that she had never been away. Richard might never have happened.

Regretting that it wasn't possible to eliminate a certain period of time, she switched on the lights and began unpacking the car. After this was completed, she found some wood and lit a fire in the lounge. She guessed that the dead ashes in the hearth were the remains of the last fire she had lit for Richard.

While the water heated for a bath, she did a quick tour of the house before plugging in the kettle to make a cup of tea. She would have something to eat later, she decided, sitting down at the kitchen table as she waited for it to boil.

She had felt no emotion when she had first arrived but it was fast catching up with her. Finding one of Richard's ties upstairs and his old bathrobe in his room downstairs, hadn't helped. She'd had only to unwisely bury her face in it for all the heartache she had been trying to escape from to come rushing back. It made her realise bitterly that, for her, there might never be any real reprieve.

But she wasn't at Cragend to escape from anything, Christine reminded herself. She had come here to try to come to terms with herself and to think seriously about her future. She may have been hoping for a miracle, such as being able to forget the man she loved, but she might achieve more, during the following days, by facing up to reality and concentrating on what might be possible, rather than on what definitely wasn't.

The following morning she was up early and she went for a walk around the loch. Having asked Jamie where Wolf was buried, she visited his grave. There was nothing to mark the spot but the huge stone Jamie had placed over it to keep predators out. Standing sadly beside it, Christine knew a terrible sense of despair for all she had lost that winter.

Back at the house, it was almost six when she thought she heard a knock on the door. She had just had a bath and she was still upstairs. After being out practically all day, she had felt in need of one. As she listened, the knocking came again and her eyes darkened apprehensively as she wondered who it could be. It wasn't the kind of night for a casual caller. Then she remembered that it could be old Jamie—why hadn't she thought of him earlier? It had been snowing all afternoon and he was probably anxious about her.

Pulling on an old pair of jeans and a sweater, she ran downstairs quickly. Without bothering to enquire who was there, doubting she would be heard above the thunderous knocking, anyway, she drew the bolts and turned the heavy key. As the door swung open, her eyes looked up to meet those of Richard Kingsley's and she received a dreadful jolt. 'You!' she gasped incredulously.

Glinting green eyes pinned her to the spot. 'I may have been greeting you in exactly the same way if I hadn't seen Jamie.' He pushed past her into the hall. 'I'm not waiting to be asked in,' he snapped, as she continued staring at him dumbly, bereft of speech. 'After all, it's my own house.'

'Yes,' she agreed hoarsely, scarcely aware of opening her mouth. She felt herself slowly disintegrating under the icy contempt in his eyes as her gaze wandered dazedly over him. His wide shoulders were encased in a thick, fur-lined leather jacket, with which he was wearing a pair of heavy cord trousers, yet, despite such protective clothing, he looked colder than she had felt an hour ago when she had come in.

'Why are you here?' she whispered, her voice sounding very like a frog's.

'Why are you?' he countered, then answered her query without waiting for her reply. 'I was in the area and decided to stay at Cragend for the night, rather than go any further when the weather turned so atrocious. If I'd known you were here it would have saved me the bother of calling on Jamie for the key.' He stared mockingly into her apprehensive blue eyes. 'We seem to be back where we started, don't we?'

'Yes and no,' she gulped, attempting to assimilate what he had told her. There seemed something odd about it somewhere, yet why should she doubt him? And she was the trespasser, not Richard. He had every right to be here, while she had no right at all. She hadn't even asked his permission.

'Is there a fire anywhere?' He turned from her sharply.

'Yes, of course.' She flushed. Shame, and a turmoil of repressed emotions made her feel ill and she tried to pull herself together. She led the way to the lounge, not knowing what else to do. When Jamie had told him she was here, it must have lessened the surprise he might otherwise have got if he'd received no warning but he clearly wasn't pleased to see her. He was grimly impassive but somewhere beneath the hard surface, she sensed a smouldering fury which threatened to consume him.

While she wondered at the strength of his reactions, he went straight to the fire. Pushing the guard aside with his foot, he held his hands out to the blaze. 'Damned heater in the car failed,' he grunted.

Christine doubted whether she would ever feel warm again. It would take more than a fire to get rid of the chill gripping her. Swallowing, she quelled a hysterical desire to laugh. She had come all the way here in order to be alone, to have time to think, only to find that the very man she most wished to avoid had practically followed her to the same place.

'Can I make you a cup of tea?' she managed to ask politely.

He turned to face her, warming his back. 'It would help—and a bath.'

'I've . . . er . . . just had one.' The colour in her cheeks deepened as she imagined him totting up the cost. 'But the water's still hot.'

With a nod he dismissed her, turning to the fire again, and, hoping he wouldn't ask any more questions, she retreated swiftly. His drawling voice caught her sharply, however, shattering her hopes before she was through the door. 'When you come back, Christine, I want to know exactly why you are here.'

All she had to do was to tell him the truth, Christine reasoned. She only need leave out the bit about loving him, the anguish of him returning to Pearl. There was nothing to be frightened of. She had committed no crime, unless being here without permission could be construed as one. She hadn't even taken unauthorised leave of absence, as she had left him a letter of resignation, or whatever it was called when a mere typist gave up her job. She didn't see how Richard could make a big thing of it. Considering everything, he should be glad to be rid of her.

Nevertheless, she felt as if she had hollow legs when she returned to the lounge. She felt even worse when she heard herself asking huskily, as she placed a tray of tea and biscuits before him, 'I thought Pearl was with you . . .?'

'You know she doesn't like Scotland,' he snapped.

Christine looked at him miserably.

'Well?' he prompted, pouring himself a large cup of steaming tea without inviting her to join him.

'Well?'

'Don't act dumb, Christine.' He bit into a biscuit as if he wished it was her neck. When she flinched, she saw a glint of what looked like evil satisfaction in his eyes.

'I—that is—my friend, Ken Granger, was getting married,' she began haltingly. 'He sent me an invitation which took a while to find me. Even so, I only decided to go to his wedding at the last minute and I had a sudden desire to spend a night or two at Cragend. I didn't think you would mind.'

'It never pays to assume.'

'I'm sorry . . .'

'Are you?' he murmured, eyes narrowed indifferently on her strained face. 'As it turns out,' he said silkily, 'it's quite convenient to find you here. As you're already working for me, you can just carry on.'

Christine gazed at him in consternation. He wouldn't have seen her resignation yet and she had no wish to explain, as she had no idea where to begin. Once started, she would be entirely at the mercy of his lethal astuteness and she could find herself humiliated unmercifully.

Obviously taking her silence for consent, he said curtly, 'You can begin by running my bath, then get my dinner. I'm ravenous.'

'If I hadn't been here,' she exclaimed with rash bitterness, 'you would have had to do without, as there was nothing in the house.'

'I came prepared.' He smiled maliciously as he delved into his pocket and tossed her his car keys. 'You'll find a bag of groceries in the boot. And while I'm having dinner,' he continued, as she grasped the keys tightly, 'you can make up the bed in the room downstairs; it's very comfortable, I grew to like it. Oh, and put a heater in the room while you're at it. If there's one thing I hate it's a cold bedroom.'

'Will that be all?' she enquired waspishly.

'For now.' He nodded magnanimously. 'But kindly hurry with my bath. I feel filthy.'

After running his bath—hoping he would drown in it—she got on with his dinner. In the boot of his car, she found thick steaks and a pile of vegetables. She cooked these and contrived a hasty sweet, deciding he could make do with tinned soup for starters. Marvelling that it had all turned out well, when her mind wasn't functioning properly, she served it to him on the same low table in front of the fire where she had given him his tea. It was too cold, he pronounced, to eat in the dining room, but again, he didn't ask her to join him.

When she set the steak in front of him, he looked it over critically and asked if there was anything to follow. When she replied there was, he told her to bring it in in half an hour.

Christine nodded without speaking. He had bathed and, like herself, was wearing a pair of jeans, but his shirt was open to the waist, revealing a breadth of dark chest it hurt her to look at. She had a sudden suspicion he had unbuttoned his shirt deliberately, then she dismissed this as ridiculous. He had probably dressed carelessly, because he was tired, rather than out of any particular desire to taunt her.

'You'd better fetch some more logs straight away,' he said as she turned to leave, which necessitated her spending the next ten minutes building the fire up while her own meal cooled in the kitchen.

Christine found that she could only nibble at her food, so it didn't really matter that it was almost past eating by the time she sat down. Not that she was allowed to sit long. Further orders shooting from the lounge had her running to and fro continually. She began to regret that she had ever come. Perhaps Richard felt better about her being here. At least he was enjoying some kind of revenge in treating her exactly like a servant. For her there was no such redress, only a mounting unhappiness.

By the time she brought his coffee in she had stopped even trying to look composed. Her face was flushed and tearful—she guessed she looked a sight, for she hadn't tidied herself since she let Richard in, but she was somehow past caring. As she stumbled with the coffee pot in front of him, he lifted arrogant brows and dared ask, in an indifferent voice, whether she was tired.

'W-would it matter?' she muttered tartly.

'No need to snap my head off,' he observed.

'I can't believe you're concerned,' she retorted, stifling a sob.

Looking at her narrowly, he said coolly, 'You can stop feeling sorry for yourself and sit down. I take it you've washed up and left your kitchen tidy?'

Mutinously she ground her small teeth together, remaining standing, suspecting that he was baiting her.

'Didn't you hear me?' he snapped, pointing to the sofa.

'Unless it's important . . .' she began.

'Christine!' Green eyes glittered.

Nervously she settled on the edge of the sofa, lifting anguished blue eyes to his face. 'I don't think we have anything more to say to one another, Richard,' she went on protesting. 'I intended to reimburse you for staying here . . .'

'You are paying for that now,' he interrupted smoothly. 'All in all, it's turning out to be very convenient.'

Did he have to be so hateful? 'If you say so,' she murmured helplessly, feeling too miserable to hit back, despite a stirring anger.

'We do have things to talk about though,' he maintained. 'So why don't you try and relax?'

She went stiffer still. 'Richard . . .!'

'So you decided to come to Scotland?' he cut in softly, ignoring her stifled plea. 'Why?'

Did he have to probe like a dentist finding where a tooth needs filling! 'I told you, Ken's wedding.'

'Was it to try and stop it?'

Her wounded glance turned into a glare. 'How could you think that? I just wanted to see him married.'

'Strange,' Richard reflected with a curling lip, 'why you didn't stay at the reception.'

The pink in her cheeks deepened. 'If I had, I shouldn't have reached Cragend before dark and I had nowhere else to go.'

'His parents offered to put you up.'

'Yes . . . but . . . Oh!' She almost passed out as she suddenly realised what he was saying. The flush on her face died to a ghastly white. 'How do you know all this?' she gasped, too shattered to even try and guess.

With a speed she found equally confusing, he was out of his chair, hauling her to her feet, poking a furious face within inches of her own colourless one. 'You little bitch!' he grated savagely. 'You didn't mind what you put me through, did you? Now you're beginning to suffer a little yourself, you don't like it. I've watched you squirming all evening. I just wish you had cared a bit more, then you might have really suffered!'

'Richard?' She gazed at him entreatingly, feeling herself shaking. 'What on earth are you talking about?'

'How you've crucified me!' he snarled between thinning lips, eyes blazing. 'How did you think I felt on arriving home, early this morning, to find your letter of resignation and to be told by Mrs Webster that you had left for Scotland, where you were to be married—yesterday!'

So Mrs Webster *had* thought that! Christine wet her shaking lips in guilty tumult. 'I told her that Ken was getting married but she's been having trouble with her hearing. I should have made sure she understood but I didn't have the time and my taxi was waiting . . .'

'I heard about her deafness and her cold,' he acknowledged less angrily, a little of the cruelty leaving the hands which held her. 'I'm afraid I didn't stop to think about it. I simply grabbed a coat and a plane and spent the day in Inverness, in a snowstorm, trying to discover where the Grangers lived.'

'But—why?' Christine whispered, unable to follow him. 'What difference could it have made to you if it had been me whom Ken had married?'

Only his glittering eyes seemed alive in a mask-like face. 'I think I would have killed you!' he said savagely. 'I was in hell and I wanted you there with me.'

Christine stifled a gasp, unable to connect this incensed, yet obviously suffering stranger with the cool, arrogant man with whom she had grown so familiar. She had thought that apart from odd surges of sexual awareness, born possibly of circumstance and loneliness, he mostly despised her. Now, something in his voice and what he was telling her, seemed to hint that there was more to it than that.

'Richard . . .' she faltered, 'Y-you said that you were just passing Cragend. You—weren't telling me the truth?'

'I was bending it,' he admitted bleakly. 'I merely left everything of importance out.'

She felt bewildered. 'Anger couldn't have brought you all the way here?'

'It wasn't anger!' Suddenly he was pulling her against him violently, burying his face in her gleaming hair. 'It was love, that devastating emotion I didn't believe in. Oh, God,' he groaned. 'What I developed for you kept on growing despite being ruthlessly denied.'

'Love?' Christine's voice trembled as she lifted her head to look at him, unable to believe what she was hearing. 'You love me . . .?'

'Yes,' he replied thickly, the burning passion in his eyes assuring her unmistakably. 'It began almost as soon as I saw you. That first morning, when you opened the door, I had never felt so mysteriously desperate to get rid of anyone in my life; then, just as inexplicably, I knew I had to keep you here at all costs. I wouldn't admit to even liking you, yet I couldn't bear to let you go.'

Lowering her gaze before the intensity of his, she whispered, 'You didn't want to like me because of Pearl?'

'No,' came the harsh reply. 'It was because you ripped through every preconceived idea I'd ever had about myself and it appalled me, what I saw.'

'But—why didn't Pearl come into it?' Christine looked up in confusion. Some of the things Harry had said came back to her but she couldn't remember clearly. 'You must have loved her to have become engaged to her?'

'No.' His voice was emphatic but his eyes darkened

and he sighed wearily. 'I didn't want to talk about this but I think I must. Pearl's husband worked for me. He was a good man but with little confidence in himself. He was always begging for more responsibility, yet he couldn't take it. This facet of his personality irritated me and I believe it was responsible for making me insist that he did a certain job in New York when he wanted to back out at the last minute. When he was killed in a road accident on the way to negotiations, I realised he must have been worrying about it and not concentrating on what he was doing and I blamed myself. Apart from business, Ben and I had been good friends, and when Pearl seemed devastated by his death, it got to be a habit, looking after her. I can't honestly say how we drifted into an engagement but I didn't realise what she was actually like until it was too late; for all that Harry kept dropping hints. The trouble with my sight was, in a way, a blessing in disguise, as, apparently she didn't want a blind husband. Otherwise, I don't know what I should have done.'

'You didn't invent the whole thing?' she asked hoarsely.

His eyes went grimmer. 'Unfortunately, no. I'll probably always have trouble with my sight, Christine. I may easily end up an old man with a white stick, so you'd better believe it.'

'Pearl left you for someone else, though,' she reminded him hesitantly.

'I don't think the other man ever existed.' Drily he echoed her own former suspicions. 'She merely used him as a loophole until she saw how things were going with me. Once she knew my eyes were all right, at least for a few more years, she thought that all she had to do was to take up where she had left off.'

'She hinted that you were lovers . . .' Christine's pale cheeks flushed.

'Never!' he exclaimed, adding grimly, 'which should have warned me. Somehow I never wanted her that way at all—and I wanted you from the beginning, my darling.'

Christine could still scarcely take it in. 'I believed, when she came, last Sunday . . .'

'I gave her dinner then sent her packing.'

'You—did?'

His mouth tightened. 'Surely you don't doubt me?'

Christine's eyes sparkled with quick resentment. 'It wouldn't be my fault if I did. I'm not a mind reader. How could I know when you didn't tell me? You didn't even tell me when you first broke your engagement, you let me go on thinking . . .'

'Oh, darling!' He caught her closer again, finding her mouth fiercely, despite her struggles. It wasn't until she was pliant in his arms, with hers wrapped tightly about him, that the pressure of his mouth eased and he resumed thickly, 'You were so young and you had met very few men. I had to give you time, at least to know your own mind. I didn't think it would be fair to take advantage of anything you felt for me when you'd had so little experience. Pearl, miraculously, it seemed, changed her mind about me but I knew if you did the same thing I wouldn't be able to bear it. That was partly why I took you to London, so that you could meet and mix with people, I was trying desperately to give you such an opportunity, when the bombshell of what Mrs Webster told me blew up in my face. I cursed the fact that I hadn't married you, asked you to marry me, anyway, while I'd had the chance.'

'Oh, Richard,' she sighed, 'if only you had.'

'Does that mean,' he had some difficulty in enunciating, 'that you will?'

'Yes.' She raised dazed, shining eyes to his, unable to deviate. Her heart racing, she said huskily, 'I love you, Richard. I tried to tell you how much in London but you wouldn't listen. And,' she added gravely, 'I have met other men. My stepmother was an actress, not that she ever did anything after she married Dad, but whenever she went to London, she thought nothing of bringing a crowd of friends back with her.'

'So,' Richard paused for a moment, 'I needn't have worried?'

'Nor need you be jealous,' she teased.

'Jealous!' he muttered thickly, staring tormentedly into her haunting blue eyes. 'You don't know how jealous I've been of anyone who looked at you—Harry, Neil Brown, Ken Granger. God, what a fool I've been!' he said hoarsely, crushing her to him. 'But I thought that I had lost you.'

His mouth found hers in a tender, worshipping kiss which swiftly changed to one of consuming passion. 'I love you,' he muttered countless times against her swollen lips.

If he had thought he had lost her, Christine had been convinced she had definitely lost him. Now such a surge of happiness and love swept through her that she clung to him too wantonly to avoid triggering off the inherent sensuality of the man holding her. Her breath caught somewhere in her stomach as she felt an answering surge of desire flooding over her, impossible to deny. For the first time in her life she wanted to belong to a man and had neither the wish nor the ability to control the force of emotions rioting through her. She couldn't find the words to tell him how she was feeling but as he continued kissing and caressing her and whispering urgently how much he wanted her, she assured him feverishly that she wanted him, too.

'I love you so much,' she murmured against his demanding mouth, making no demure when, like a man driven beyond the limits of endurance, he lifted her, carrying her through to his bedroom. It was only a few yards away and he laid her in the middle of the bed. The room was warm but the heat coursing through Christine's veins would have kept her warm if it hadn't been.

He stood staring down at her, his hands clenched by the sides of his lean, muscular body, oblivious of everything but her glowing dark beauty. Her tight jeans clung to her narrow waist, the enticing curve of her hips, while her sweater did nothing to hide the fullness of her rounded breasts.

His breath rasped and suddenly the bed dipped with his weight as he came down beside her, gathering her to him again. 'Christine, darling, are you sure?' he asked thickly. 'I want you so much that it's agony, but I'm willing to wait—even if it kills me.'

Christine's heart pounded. 'A lot of good you would be to me then.'

She had managed a teasing remark but found it impossible to produce a matching smile. Richard's hands framed her face, his thumbs making gentle circles under her chin. When she trembled and swallowed nervously, he said, 'Don't be afraid, darling. I won't hurt you.'

'I don't mind, I love you,' she assured him.

She had a brief glimpse of smouldering eyes burning into hers before his mouth descended, parting her lips with an expertise that made her feel as if she was drowning. Her emotions seared and soared as his mouth left a trail of fire over her face and throat, while the heat of his hands under her sweater sent a wild kind of weakness flowing right through her. Swiftly, he began to undress her but Christine had no clear recollection of him doing so as complete awareness of what was happening to her faded.

He must have removed his own clothing as well, for suddenly they were both naked and clinging together. Any fear Christine had felt dissolved in the warmth of their hungry bodies. Her senses reeled at the touch of his strong hands on her supple, responsive flesh and she couldn't suppress the shudder of desire that shook her as his mouth found and closed over a taut nipple.

She loved him desperately; her voice broke as she tried to tell him how much. He went on kissing her, soothing her, caressing her, until she was only conscious of his soft murmurings and the sensuous heat of his mouth.

His hands roamed her body with a hard, probing intimacy, yet she caught brief glimpses of a tenderness which reassured her. When their passion became a raging storm, no longer containable, apprehension returned to Christine fleetingly as he moved on top of her and her innocence momentarily protested. But, as if sensing this, Richard's lips gentled until her raging desire conquered her fears again.

The devastating force with which he took her brought a transient pain which she scarcely noticed, before a rushing flood of incredible rapture. As he moved inside her, after the first sharp halt of his entry, Christine was overwhelmed by feelings of such incomprehensible intensity that she felt she might shatter. She was startled by the explosive quality of her own sensuality as her body responded with increasing fierceness to his. When something seemed to snap in him, releasing a certain savagery, she responded with a matching urgency which asked for no mercy and appeared to remove the last of his restraint. Within seconds he was possessing her yielding softness completely, taking her with him until they were both whirling mindlessly in some magical place, at the mercy of violent waves of such intense pleasure that it was a long time before either of them could speak.

Slowly, Christine became aware of Richard's heart still pounding against her own and his arms still around her. 'I love you,' he muttered hoarsely, green eyes devouring her. 'I've never known anything like this.'

Christine tightened her own arms around him shyly, letting him know that she understood. It was all new to her, yet incredibly wonderful. After a few minutes she felt him harden against her again and his hand slid to the side of her breast.

'God!' he groaned, drawing a sharp breath at his own vulnerability. 'The sooner we are married the better. I don't think I'll ever be satisfied.'

'It was the first time for me,' she whispered, without knowing why.

'I realised that, sweetheart.' He kissed her lovingly. 'I should be ashamed, but I can only worship you more for giving yourself to me. I want you to know I'll never betray your trust.'

He murmured passionately, as their arms tightened simultaneously, 'We will be married as soon as possible. I'm shelving a lot of future contracts because of my eyes. That's what I've been doing in New York this week, though I haven't told anyone here yet. I'm retaining most of my London staff, though they will have to carry on a lot of the time without me. I intend spending most of my time with my wife—if she will let me?'

Christine kissed him and caressed his cheek gently. 'I don't think she will have any objections.'

Suddenly he sobered, his green eyes almost grim. 'You don't mind that, one day, I may not be able to see you?'

'Don't you think that it's a bit late to ask me that?' she teased, then, just as soberly, 'oh, darling, I'll always love you and want to be with you, whatever happens. You don't have to worry.'

'My little love,' he groaned, holding her fiercely. 'I'm sorry that I treated you so badly but you don't know the hell I've been through, loving you and realising that Pearl was a mistake I might have to live with. Until she released me, I thought I was going crazy, yet even when she did, I felt forced to go on using her in order to protect you from yourself. I thought that you had scarcely met anyone but Granger and me. Even if I had known that you hadn't been completely isolated, I would have wanted to protect your innocence. And now look what's happened.'

'I have no regrets,' she whispered softly, with an enchanting blush. 'All that matters is that we love each other and want to be together always.'

'I'm going to be a very demanding husband,' he

said thickly, kissing her deeply again, as she snuggled closer.

Desire stirred inside Christine swiftly, as his hand urgently caressed the bare curve of her back while his mouth wandered tenderly over her hot face. Richard loved her and all her heartache had incredibly disappeared to be replaced by a wonderful feeling of warm happiness which she knew would survive forever.

She let a wave of exultation sweep right through her. 'Just as long as you don't mind having a very demanding wife,' she murmured shamelessly, before being thoroughly made love to for her pains.

Can anyone tame Tamara?

Life is one long party for the outrageous Tamara.

Not for her wedded bliss and domesticity.

Fiercely independent and determined to stay that way, her one goal is to make a success of her acting career.

Then, during a brief holiday with her sister, Tamara's life is turned upside down by Jake DeBlais, man of the world and seducer of women…

Discover love in full bloom in this exciting sequel to Arctic Rose, by Claire Harrison.

Available from May 1986.

Price £2.25.

WORLDWIDE